"I'm sorry, Angie, really—"

"I know." She couldn't look at him and stay focused, so she made herself let his hand go. A few more inches between them would be a good idea, too. She couldn't make her body scoot away, so she grabbed on to harsh realities to create the distance she needed. "Running around town with a baby she's not supposed to have might just get Maggie killed."

"Then help me find her before anyone else does." The desperation in Tony's expression drew her in even further. "Help me protect my niece."

She gave up her fight not to put her arms around him. Focusing on only the job had never seemed more impossible. Tony's initial resistance melted into the kind of rib-crushing hug that confirmed how much he'd needed the comfort she was offering.

No man had ever felt more right in her arms.

Dear Reader,

We live our lives. We work hard. We look at the world around us, decide what's next and strike a new course. Life goes on, and so do we. Most of the time.

But a day's hard work sometimes reveals less about where we want to go, and instead mirrors what we've left behind. The past we refuse to deal with. The disappointments that never really go away.

The Runaway Daughter takes us back to Oakwood, Georgia, and to the exciting small-town lives of the Rivers family. Tony Rivers is a sheriff's deputy. A good ol' boy who's the life of every party. It's either laugh or look back, and Tony never looks back. Chief Deputy Angie Carter, who's working hard to forget her own disappointments, becomes his unwilling accomplice as he fights to protect his brother's child.

Tony's finished with losing the people he cares about, and he can't keep his niece safe without Angie's help. Looks as if the past is tired of being ignored, and so is the attraction that's been brewing between these two for months.

I love to hear from my readers. Be sure to let me know what you think of *The Runaway Daughter* at www.annawrites.com.

Sincerely,

Anna

THE RUNAWAY DAUGHTER

Anna DeStefano

HARLEQUIN®

TORONTO • NEW YORK • LONDON
AMSTERDAM • PARIS • SYDNEY • HAMBURG
STOCKHOLM • ATHENS • TOKYO • MILAN • MADRID
PRAGUE • WARSAW • BUDAPEST • AUCKLAND

ISBN 0-373-71329-0

THE RUNAWAY DAUGHTER

Books by Anna DeStefano

HARLEQUIN SUPERROMANCE

1234–THE UNKNOWN DAUGHTER
1280–A FAMILY FOR DANIEL

Andrew—For all you've been, every precious day you give, and the future shining in each beautiful smile.

TOA—You were there for the very first sentence. May every blessing given be returned hundredfold. This is your year, sweetie!

Tanya—To believe, to dream, to laugh. Your friendship is the well I return to time and again. The stars are yours, my friend. Breathe deep and enjoy the ride.

CHAPTER ONE

I SHOULDN'T BE DOING this.

Oakwood Chief Deputy Angie Carter had been trying to talk herself out of trouble, and the dingy pool hall, for over an hour.

The voice in her head knew what it was talking about. She'd let things go too far, which made her an idiot. Playing with fire like this would only get her singed.

But tonight, her *let's be reasonable* voice wasn't having its say.

Her hand slid higher, on a mission she couldn't stop. Up miles of strong muscles and across the soft, warm cotton that covered the chest leaning into hers. His arms pulled her more solidly against him. Her fingers tangled in his dark brown hair.

I shouldn't be doing this....

Oh yes, you should.

"Mmm." His warm lips nibbled from her ear down her neck. "So this is what a lady sheriff tastes like."

"Not…" She gasped as his hands skimmed the undersides of her breasts. "Not the new sheriff yet. But still—"

His mouth settled over hers, swallowing the second thoughts he wouldn't let her finish. At thirty-five she was ten years his senior, more experienced both in the department and in life. With more at stake. And he…he was too young, and too handsome, and far too good at kissing to heed warnings she'd stopped listening to hours ago.

I'm not going to do this….

"N…No." She pushed away from the wall of muscle pressed against her, the craving to lose herself in its heat nearly her undoing.

Hell yeah, she wanted this. She'd wanted it for months. But what she wanted and the crumbs life actually threw her way were two different things. A gem of reality she'd learned three years ago, when the life she'd had by the tail had crashed and burned around her.

She pulled away. A traitorous sigh escaped when his lips grazed her cheek. "No more. We shouldn't… We can't—"

"Feels a lot like we can to me." His eyes twinkled with mischief, but he loosened his hold and let her slide to the far corner of the booth.

She glanced around the shadowy bar, relieved that

the Eight Ball was deserted. It was late at night in the middle of a work week, and every other sane person in town was home in bed.

"No one's here to see your fall from grace, darlin'." He followed her gaze. His deep chuckle made her ache to pull him closer again. He looked too amazing in his Wranglers and vintage Harley-Davidson T-shirt. Too much like something she could get used to wanting.

Why did he have to find fun in everything he did? Why did she have to envy him the talent?

The lightness he brought to every situation—even the tough ones they often faced on the job, or as they did volunteer work with some of the more mixed-up kids at Oakwood's youth center—was a constant temptation. Terrifying was a better word for the way his laughter drew her in.

Why hadn't they left well enough alone? People didn't stumble over friendships like theirs every day. He was easy to like, easy to hang out with, this man who'd cornered the market on forgetting the past— the very thing she longed to be a pro at herself.

Then she'd gone and let herself want more.

"Tonight was a mistake," she sputtered.

A real stupid move, and she wasn't stupid.

Not anymore.

"Mistakes aren't always bad, Carter." He used her

last name, the way officers addressed each other. Like a peer on the force. A good buddy.

Only this was the buddy she'd just been crawling all over. And he never called her *Carter* in that lazy, sinful way when they were on duty.

She applied the back of her hand to her lips and wiped. Sipped her now-warm beer. If she couldn't taste him anymore, she'd have a shot at damage control.

"I'm ten years older than you are."

"Damn straight! I like my women more experienced and ready to teach me somethin'."

"Don't be an ass." If whatever this was between them was about sexual experience, he was a dirty old man, and she was the jailbait.

He tipped back his own longneck bottle and raised an eyebrow at her get-real glare.

"Okay," he conceded. "Maybe I like a challenge. Pushing limits can be a whole lot of fun."

"If getting fired is the kind of limit you're looking to blow, then I'm your girl."

"No one's getting fired." His settled his shoulders against the cushioned seat with a thump. "Lighten up, will ya?" There wasn't much punch behind his complaint. Without looking her in the eye, he toyed with the label he'd shredded off his beer. "Why is everything so damn serious with you? You've got so much *moody* bottled up inside, you feel enough for ten people. Probably why we're such a good fit." He chuckled. "Lord knows, there's no other woman in town who'd get me within ten feet of talking about feelings."

And there it was.

That hint of something beneath the good ol' boy facade.

Tony Rivers played *Mr. Good Times* like a Hollywood star. But turbulent currents ran beneath all that practiced nonchalance. There were glimpses of passion and determination, always at the most unexpected times. A sense of responsibility and duty to others that contradicted both his party lifestyle and his youth. A spark of intensity flashing behind come-here-baby brown eyes that sucked her in even quicker than his smile.

And he was poking fun at *her* moodiness?

"Serious is the only way my life works." How she made it through the day. "I work hard, and I don't make careless mistakes like this."

"Not being the most controlled person in the room might be fun for a change. Why not give it a chance?" His lips curled playfully. "Who knows, darlin'. You might just like a bit of carelessness in your life."

"Carelessness is something I can't afford to develop a taste for. I'm leaving." She cringed at the schoolgirl waver in her voice.

She stood, her frazzled nerves screaming to sprint, not walk, toward the door. His hand caught her wrist, and her skin tingled with excitement, same as any other time they touched.

"I'm sorry." All teasing drained from his voice. "Look, you're right. This was a mistake. The last thing I want to do is cause you trouble, but…"

His unfinished sentence vibrated between them. Words beyond good friends and easy camaraderie. Words that would shove the craziness they'd started tonight over the invisible line between careless and too far.

How many times had they almost had this conversation? How many months had she let this drag on, as they flirted with the ugly way this could turn out for both of them?

Against her better judgment, she let her gaze caress his face. The bar's dim lighting and the uncharacteristic worried expression Tony wore had produced a sight few in town would believe. Roughness edged the jaw of Oakwood's golden boy and shadows eclipsed his nonstop cheerfulness. The restraint it took not to smooth away his frown made her ache.

They'd only talked about his parents once or twice, but she knew enough, and had guessed plenty more. He'd lost them both too young—his mom, when she'd split only a year after he was born; then his dad, killed while on the job as sheriff six years later. And ever since, he'd made a point of not letting himself want anything or anyone he couldn't walk away from with a shrug and smile. Keeping everyone at a comfortable distance while he was the life of the party was more Tony's style. A warped world view Angie couldn't help but appreciate. She hid behind her man's uniform and her career. He overindulged in shallow relationships with women. The end result was the same.

Sometimes she wasn't sure who was lonelier.

"Let me go, Tony."

"Come on, don't leave like this. It won't happen again." His grip on her arm tightened. "We see each other at work nearly every day. You've been friends with my family for years. We're going to have to figure out what to do when—"

"There's nothing to figure out. There is no *when!*" She pulled free and slammed the door shut on her indecision. "And you're damn right this will never happen again. I'm your superior officer, Deputy Rivers. That means hands off, for both of us."

She made herself walk out of the Eight Ball. She didn't need this. She didn't need him.

She'd rebuilt her life from nothing. She'd regained a speck of the peace she'd thought she'd lost for good. Her job as a deputy, and then chief, had saved her. Her run for sheriff was the future.

It was enough.

It had to be.

"ARE YOU TELLING ME you *want* a lady sheriff?" Deputy Martin Rhodes asked with a sideways glance. "You've got to be kidding!"

"Would that be so bad?" Tony ducked his head farther into his locker.

It was a little after three o'clock; he and Martin were rolling off their morning shift, and all the man wanted to talk about was their chief deputy.

Perfect.

"Angie's a good cop." Tony kept his mind focused on the job, and *only* the job. "Everybody knows that. She's been chief for three years now."

"Yeah, but that's with your brother overseeing things." Martin was practically pouting. An alarming sight on the burly man, who looked better suited for a career in professional wrestling than small-town law enforcement. "Eric is old-school, like I hear your daddy was. Laid back, until he has to bust some balls. Then he's the point guy you want leading the charge. Angie… Well, you know how she is."

Tony's grunt said he didn't know a thing about their chief deputy, which was the God's-honest truth.

He fished in his locker for street clothes to replace the sweaty uniform he'd shucked off. Not even interested in a shower before he dressed and left, he stripped down to his boxers and let the frustration of all he and his riding partner hadn't accomplished that day wash over him. Drugs were leaking into Oakwood and the surrounding county. From where, the department wasn't sure yet. But they had damn well better figure it out.

Their sleepy little corner of Georgia had the unfortunate distinction of being strategically located on a major north-south interstate running from the Carolinas down through Florida. A convenient crossroads, as it turned out, through which producers of the latest narcotic commodity of choice could network with southeastern buyers and dealers.

Crystal meth—inexpensive and instantly addictive—had wormed a filthy trail through Oakwood over the last year. And each of the nine deputies in the department was committed to finding the dealers and their runners before any more damage was done. Before any more people were hurt. Just last month, the town's first drive-by shooting had resulted in an unknown man riddled with bullets and left to die on a street corner not two blocks from the Oakwood Youth Center. No ID. No one came forward to claim the body. No clue to who'd killed him.

Tony had been on duty since six, after a near-sleepless night, hunting a mobile drug lab one of Martin's contacts had fingered as a *sure-thing* tip. Only the lab had vanished before they'd gotten there, leaving Tony and Martin roaming dirt roads on the outskirts of town, searching for an unmarked four-wheel-drive SUV with a trailer attached. They'd found nothing for their efforts but rising July temperatures and more questions. Like how the local drug network always managed to stay one step ahead of the department.

And if trudging through mosquitoes and steamy weather hadn't been bad enough, his partner's relentless preoccupation with Angie's bid to become the next sheriff kept veering into downright uncomfortable territory.

"You know she's not right for the job." Martin could make a bulldog look wishy-washy. "I don't care if she's the mayor's pet project, or if she and Eric are friends. He's got no business pushing for her election, when—"

"My brother's not pushing for anything." Tony slammed his locker shut. Catching his friend's shock at his uncharacteristic outburst, he shrugged and rifled through his duffel bag. "The people in town will make up their own minds when they vote. And Angie will have the city council to answer to if she's elected. That's a month down the road. Why get your panties in a wad about it now?"

Right back atcha, Rivers.

Defending Angie to anyone in the department was stupid. The woman could take care of herself. Yeah, she wanted this election badly. But there was no crime in that, even if she did seem downright desperate lately.

Desperate.

An image from last night barreled into him. An instant replay of Angie, all soft brown hair, hot green eyes and desperation, pushing away from the sexiest kiss he'd ever been on the receiving end of. The look on her face had hinted that *he* could be the center of her world. *He* could be what she wanted most. The answer to whatever she was searching for so desperately.

He swallowed a curse. Angie had made it clear anything beyond friendship and strictly business was a nonstarter. Obsessing about memories of how good they were together was pointless.

Thank God!

No more wondering what made her tick. No more circling the woman, looking for a way in like a teenager on hormone overload. It was time to shrug off Martin's nonsense and thoughts of Angie and drive his tired ass home.

"This town's not ready for a woman sheriff," his

partner insisted. "Not *that* woman, anyway. The department's not ready. I don't care how nice the legs are under those man-pants she always wears."

Well, hell.

"The lady's legs aren't any of your business." Some things even an easygoing guy couldn't let slide. Tony laced his sneakers so tight, it was a wonder he could still feel his toes. "Angie's pulled her weight around here, and then some, for as long as my brother. Gender's got nothing to do with being sheriff, unless your problem's with women on the force in general."

"I'm not the one with the problem." Martin's face reddened. "It's our chief deputy who's got herself a problem. Sure Angie's climbed her way to the top. Hell, she's a regular poster child for equal opportunity. And she's an okay cop, when she's not distracted by press conferences with the mayor, or brown-nosing your brother. But being in charge takes more than that pair of balls she's been trying to grow. She's burned a lot of bridges, and she's been promoted over a lot of good men who were in line before her. Every time the mayor shakes her hand and treats her like one of his family, she's taking credit for the hard work of every other deputy in the department. And a lot of us don't appreciate it. That ain't going to change because she charms herself a new title."

Tony could only stare. Angie took her commitment to protecting the citizens of Oakwood as seriously as any of the men. She was in law enforcement to serve her fellow citizens, not just to build a career. And she was working around the clock like the rest of the deputies, fighting to stomp out the drugs ripping at their small-town world. Yet the resentment toward her from a handful of the men grew stronger by the day.

Martin nodded as his words sunk in. "Your brother and the mayor's influence might get her elected. But it's a whole different ball game after that. If the woman isn't careful, she'll look for someone to watch her back one day, and there might not be anyone lining up to do the job."

"That's the most ignorant load of bullshit I've ever heard." Tony pushed himself off the bench. The nasty feelings brewing inside him since leaving the Eight Ball alone last night boiled over. "Angie Carter's the finest cop in this county. She'd take a bullet for your sorry ass without blinking an eye, though at the moment I can't think of a single good reason why."

He stepped forward. The several inches in height he had on Martin crowded the heavier man against the lockers.

"I don't ever want to hear you or anyone else threaten not to cover her back, you hear me?"

"What's wrong with you, man?" Martin used his forearm to shove some distance between them. "I didn't mean nothin'. Besides, why are you so determined to defend her all of a sudden? You're downright cagey every time her name comes up. I even heard a rumor you and Carter might have something goin'—"

"Don't finish that sentence." Tony realized he was pointing a finger in his friend's face. Overreacting to a wad of harmless, locker room griping at the end of a long, hot morning.

All because he'd felt like pounding something for weeks.

"Problem, boys?"

Eric rounded the row of lockers closest to them.

"No problem," Tony and Martin said in unison, neither breaking eye contact. Neither moving a muscle.

Eric cleared his throat, a nonverbal bid for their undivided attention. Tony blinked first, fed up with the whole scene. When the hell had he started caring so much what anyone thought about anything? He grabbed his duffel bag from where he'd dropped it beneath the bench, and headed for the door.

"I was just leaving," he mumbled as he strode past his brother.

They were having a special dinner at home that night, and he needed a couple hours of sleep before he could manage another round of *everything's okay*.

It was a send-off of sorts. Eric and his new bride were heading for New York in the morning—on a belated honeymoon and to scout out places to live while their nineteen-year-old daughter attended NYU.

Tony's family was moving away. Evaporating. Only a year after his spunky, long-lost niece and sister-in-law had dropped back into their lives, and then undergone delicate, lifesaving surgeries. In another month, two at the most, they'd be gone.

He found himself scouting the deserted hallway for something to kick.

The over-the-top impulse had him chuckling to himself. *Damn, man, you're losing it. Suck it up and cut the melodrama.*

Eric, Carrinne and Maggie deserved whatever happiness they could grab. No way was he standing in their way, even if he was already missing them like hell.

He felt Eric's stare track him as he walked away. He'd only made it halfway down the hall when he heard footsteps approach from behind.

"Hold up," his brother called.

Tony hefted his duffel higher and kept moving.

"I said hold up." Eric grabbed Tony's arm and yanked him around.

"Not now, okay!"

The look on Eric's face insisted that *now* was exactly when it was going to be.

Eric had always been more of father than a brother to Tony. The man had given up a chunk of his life after their parents were both gone, to make sure Tony had one of his own. Tony's respect for Eric's sacrifices was rock solid. His brother was as steady as they came. Regardless of the crap life threw his way, he stuck it out, muscled through and made things work. And he took nothing more seriously than he did his family, especially after all they'd been through this last year. And that, Tony admired most of all. Squaring his shoulders, he made himself stay put.

This conversation was long overdue. If it hadn't been for the drug mess eating up every speck of Eric's free time, Tony wouldn't have been able to avoid him this long. He deserved the ass-chewing, and he was done making his brother hunt him down to do it.

"Suppose you tell me what the hell's going on between you and Angie?" Eric crossed his arms, digging in for the duration.

CHAPTER TWO

ERIC ALREADY KNEW the answers to his question, enough of them anyway. Still, he wouldn't believe it until he heard it from Tony's mouth.

His brother hooking up with Angie Carter. Of all the careless, harebrained things—

"Nothing's going on." Tony's expression was a careful study in innocence. Same as when he'd been younger and Eric had caught him in one of the half-truths kids clung to rather than facing the music for what they'd done.

"Then I suppose you were only helping Angie fish something out of her eye last night at the Eight Ball."

Hearing the latest rumors, Eric had been hunting for his brother after shift change.

Tony's duffel hit the ground. He propped his fists on his hips, where his cutoff T-shirt didn't quite meet his raggedy gym shorts.

"Nothing happened last night," he said evenly.

"That's not what I heard."

"From who?"

"Now why do you think that would matter?" Eric scratched the back of his neck and did his best imitation of their old man. "I don't care where the story started, and even less whether it's true or not."

"Then what the hell do you want from me?"

"How anyone could have gotten the crazy notion that you and my chief deputy have been going out for weeks, that's what I'm more concerned about."

Tony's gaze dropped to the floor.

"Damn." Eric hissed in a breath. "I never figured either of you for being stupid."

Tony looked him square in the eye then, man-to-man.

On the force, he had grown into the responsibility Eric knew he was capable of. No father could be prouder. But the kid still hadn't shaken off the past. His antics away from the department made him the star of every party, but the good times never seemed to follow him home. And his behavior spoke more of running these days, than of having fun.

Then he and Angie had started hanging out at the youth center, spending more and more time together off the job. Which should have been a good thing. If the kid was getting serious with anyone but their chief deputy, Eric would be all for it. But why Angie?

"We've been going out for a few beers after work the last couple of weeks." Tony winced. "Shooting some pool. Talking. Last night…just happened, okay. I don't know… One minute we were blowing off steam, same as usual. She'd scratched breaking a new rack of balls, and I was giving her a hard time about it. The next thing I knew…we were in the booth, and she was smiling up at me and…" He shrugged again. "The place was empty. There was no one there to see."

"Nowhere in this town is empty enough to keep something like you and Angie going after each other under wraps."

"We weren't going after anything. It was a kiss, and it wasn't her idea. I initiated it, and she ended it. We both know we're better off just friends. It was a mistake…." Tony's face flushed with anger. "And anyone who says any different needs to keep his mouth shut, or I'll shut it for him."

Holy hell.

Eric buried his hands in the back pockets of his jeans. Tony might have convinced himself that he and Angie were all about nothing, but Eric wasn't buying it. His baby brother was falling for about the only woman in town the kid couldn't have. A woman who, incidentally, could use a good time or two.

"You're tangling with a line you can't cross, son." Eric gifted his brother with the same look he'd once used to explain the birds and the bees. "Angie's a superior officer. If you don't care what something like this would do to your career, think about hers. She's up for sheriff, with Mayor Henderson and half the town breathing down her neck every waking hour. She's fought for this chance for years."

"I know that, but—"

"And even if she wasn't my chief, she's not like the other women you date, who like things as fast and loose as you do. After the way Freddie Peters messed Angie up, you can't play her, then move on to someone else. I'm not even sure she's dated since the man broke off their engagement. That was three years ago."

"I know all about Freddie Peters. Angie told me the whole story. Give me some credit. I wouldn't hurt her like that bastard did. Not for the world!"

They'd had a heart-to-heart about her ex-fiancé? *Just friends my ass.*

"End this before it gets serious," Eric warned, wondering if he wasn't already too late.

"There's nothing to end." His brother's chin lifted.

"Bull."

"There's nothing going—"

"I don't want to hear any more." He wished he had the time, but today he was fresh out. "I'm getting on a plane with Carrinne in the morning, and there's enough to worry about around here without your libido stirring up trouble in my department. Another kid OD'd early this morning. Travis Reynolds—Dawson and Lettie's oldest. They found him at home. Drove him to the hospital. No one called the department until the E.R. doc coded him DOA."

"Damn." Tony's expression hardened. "Was it—"

"Meth," Eric confirmed, raging inside at the toll drugs were taking on their town.

Methamphetamine was a designer drug, its trade ideally built to lure in teen dealer-wannabes. Local kids with their own cars, too little money and too much time on their hands. It was easy to manufacture, easy to score and hugely profitable to anyone who needed fast cash. Nothing the department had tried had made a dent in Oakwood's growing drug culture. And no one spent more time with the kids who were most at risk than Tony. The teens who wandered in and out of the Oakwood Youth Center were his pet project.

"The ME confirmed it was the same grade of stuff as last Christmas," Eric added. A kid the next county over had celebrated New Year's early with a buddy who'd talked him into trying meth. The fifteen-year-old hadn't lived to see January. "More than likely, from the same supplier."

"I saw Travis at the center the other day," Tony

said, the fury in his eyes tinged with loss. "He and some of the other boys kicked my ass at pool."

Travis Reynolds had been a cocky kid who'd taken pride in his no-good rep: skipping school, getting booted off the football team for bad grades. He'd even been arrested last month for DUI, by Tony of all people, and his license had been pulled. But he'd been joyriding with Garret Henderson that night, the mayor's kid. A little mayorly finagling and pressure from the city council had kept the boys out of jail.

Travis had been back on the streets in less than forty-eight hours. Eric wasn't the only one who'd figured it was just a matter of time before the teen self-destructed again. But no one had expected it would end this way. Least of all the shocked and grieving parents Eric had left at the hospital.

"What a waste." He rubbed a hand across his face and refocused on his brother's own foray into reck-lessness. "And Angie's going to have her hands full dealing with the fallout while I'm gone. So do her and yourself a favor. Steer clear of the woman outside of the job."

"Eric, it's not what you think—"

"Angie deserves better than one of your twenty-four-hour specials."

"I know that."

"Then keep your hands off!"

Eric headed for his office and the mound of paperwork he had to finish before leaving to scout out the future he, his wife and their daughter had been waiting a lifetime to start. He hated the idea of leaving Oakwood now, even for a few weeks. The timing sucked. But he trusted his people to watch over the town. His deputies knew how to do their jobs. They were professionals.

Most of the time, anyway.

Had his brother and his chief deputy lost their minds?

"DRUGS?" MAGGIE RIVERS asked Claire Morton.

They'd moved their whispered conversation into the girls' bathroom at the Oakwood Youth Center. Anything to avoid the posse of teenage boys, Garret Henderson included, who wouldn't stop talking about Travis Reynolds overdosing. The mayor's son always thrived on sharing every gory detail he overheard from his dad.

Claire's baby was in dire need of a diaper change, so she and Maggie had jumped at the excuse to get lost.

"Are you sure Sam's dealing?" Maggie asked her friend.

"He's doing more than that. I think he's supplying the stuff to half the county. Where else would he be getting the money for the new car, and the apartment and all the electronic junk he's got lying around every-where?" Claire shoved her frizzy red hair away from her face and yanked at the plastic tape holding the diaper on a wiggling baby Max. The plastic unfolded from the baby's bottom, revealing more mess than a seven-month-old should be capable of making.

Maggie couldn't keep from covering her nose.

"Oh, that's not right!" She tried breathing through her mouth. It didn't help.

"Peaches." Claire went to work with a wad of baby wipes. She looked like she wanted to race Maggie for the door. "I'm trying solid foods, and this happens every time he eats strained peaches."

"Then stop giving them to him." Desperate to do something to help, Maggie fished for a fresh diaper in her friend's oversize bag.

She lifted out an Elmo-emblazoned plastic panty. A small baggie came with it, slipping off the diaper onto the cracked, fake-marble surface of the vanity. The white powder inside could have been formula. But the speed at which her friend snatched the baggie off the counter put a swift end to that theory.

"You see?" Claire waved it fiercely in the air between them. She left Maggie to hold the baby as she stomped to the nearest stall and flushed the bag, contents and all, down the toilet. "Sam thinks he's hiding it from me. There's never anything like this in the apartment. But I found more between the seats of his car the other day. He wouldn't tell me what it was— just that it was none of my business. Now it's in Max's things. I think...I think Sam might have even been selling the stuff that killed Travis. I saw them talking together the other day, all secret-like. And Travis called Sam's cell phone yesterday morning."

Maggie stared as her friend returned her attention to the baby she'd made with Sam Walker, one of the shadiest characters in Oakwood. She had to keep her cool for her friend's sake. Claire had never thought she was a goody-goody, like some of the other kids, just because her dad was the sheriff and her uncle a deputy. Now wasn't the time to prove her friend wrong and start nagging about the law.

Besides, she'd heard worse back home in New York, where she'd lived with her mom until a year ago. It hadn't been hard to pick out the druggies and the dealers in her high school in Manhattan. Even though she'd gone to a specialized math and science school with some of the smartest kids in the country, the drug culture had been accepted as a way of life. Moving to picturesque Georgia to live with her newly discovered father, Maggie had expected things to be different. Simpler somehow, more homespun.

But it hadn't taken long to recognize the familiar

patterns. The half lives being lived by people, many of them teens her age or younger, who fed their habits in secret, or so they thought. But the secrets were getting harder to hide. Her dad's deputies kept raiding places all over town, trying to bust things up. But nothing was working.

And now Claire's boyfriend was the ring leader?

"There were all these people at the apartment when Max and I got home last night." Her friend hefted the now clean smelling baby onto her shoulder and pushed at the hair falling into her worried blue eyes. "I didn't know many of them. I never do. It seems like it's a new bunch every time, except for one or two of the local guys Sam keeps telling me to forget about seeing there. And there are the endless cell-phone calls. The beepers going off all the time. Then Sam or one of his goons disappears, and it's hours before I see them again. They keep talking about some kind of shack over on his mom's property near Pineview. They're storing who knows what there. And one of the guys last night had a gun. I swear, Maggie, I've never been so scared in my life."

"If Sam's running the local drug scene, you can't stay with him, Claire. It's not safe, for you or for Max. You've got to get out of there."

And you've got to tell somebody, but Maggie didn't dare say the words out loud. Claire was so freaked, no way would she talk to Maggie's dad or any grown-up. Not until she was free of Sam.

"Get out where? Like I can find some place to stay without going to Sam's family. And those people are bad as he is. I think he's bankrolling most of them with the money he's making. No way would they take my side against him. They wouldn't let me walk away with Max, either."

"You're always complaining that Sam never spends any time with the baby." Maggie smoothed a hand over the downy fluff on Max's head. She and her dad would never get back the years when neither of them had known the other existed. Every new day was a scramble to make up for what they'd missed. How could Sam not care about his own kid? "I hate to say it, but I doubt Sam's going to stop you two from leaving."

"Maybe not, but his family would. The Walkers are like some kind of backwoods clan—nobody takes what's theirs. And they're all over the place," Claire added with a touch of envy.

She'd hit town as a runaway, leaving behind parents she said had wanted to control her life and tell her what to do. She'd been on her way to somewhere bigger like Atlanta. Someplace you could start over and make a new beginning with nothing, not even a high-school diploma. But then she'd hooked up with Sam Walker, and the guy's anything-goes, get-the-most-from-today line had made Oakwood look really good.

Now, a year and a half later, she and Max were trapped in a no-win situation worse than what she'd left behind in Virginia.

"Sam's mama's not going to let this baby out of her sight," Claire added.

"What does Betty Walker have to do with it? Max is yours."

"And Sam is hers. My job is to make her son happy, and take care of her grandson. If she got wind I was even thinking of leaving, the family would take Max from me and worry about making it look legal later."

"Then you'd go to the police. My dad—"

"The Walkers could make Max disappear before your dad got to them. I have no one here, Maggie. My parents don't even know I had a baby. And I'm not sure they'd help, even if they did. I've got to forget all the stuff going on in the apartment and make the best of it. At least until Max is older. Maybe then if I take him away, I can leave him with someone while I work."

And that was the argument Maggie kept banging her head against, every time she tried to talk her friend into walking away from her baby's father. Claire believed she was completely helpless. Completely dependent. Sam and his family made sure of it.

"Can… Can you talk with Sam about it?" Maggie fought not to tell her friend she was nuts for even thinking of sleeping one more night in that apartment. "Maybe he'll agree to do whatever he's doing somewhere else. There has to be some other place he can…you know, do business with people."

What was she saying! Sam Walker had to be stopped.

But Claire was already shaking her head, her eyes clouding with tears. "I hardly say anything to him anymore. The baby's crying all night, and he's tired of Max's stuff being all over the apartment when he has people over. I don't even think he wants us there, except his mama'd hit the roof if he turned us out. And I think…I think I heard him and those guys talking about that drive-by shooting that happened last month. I…I think Sam was involved somehow. Maybe that guy who died even worked for him. I'm scared, Maggie. I…" A tear trickled down. "I don't know what to do."

"The drive-by's all my dad and my uncle talk about. Nothing like that's ever happened here before. It's got everyone in town messed up worrying. Claire—" She grasped her friend's elbow. "You've got to get away from Sam."

"I can't. Where would I go?"

"Let me talk to my dad. He'll know what to do."

Her *dad.* Maggie's chest grew tight, same as every time she thought how lucky she was to have her mom, and now her dad and Uncle Tony in her life. Even crusty old LeJeune was growing on her. Her Oakwood family took care of each other like nobody's business, the part of her newfound southern heritage she liked best. To people down here, *family* meant fighting to the death for the people you loved.

But Claire had no one to fight for her but scummy Sam.

And me. She has me.

"Don't you dare tell Sheriff Rivers," her friend warned. "No cops. They'd want to question Sam and his family. They'd take Max away from me, 'cause I have no way to take care of him without Sam's money, then the Walkers—"

"My dad wouldn't do that—"

"I swear, Maggie. If you tell anyone about this—"

"Okay! I won't."

"If you do, I'll never speak to you ag—"

The bathroom door swung open.

Claire sucked in the rest of her threat.

"Hey girls." Angie Carter's smile lost some of its customary gusto as she absorbed their stunned silence. "Everything okay?"

"Everything's fine." Claire grabbed the diaper bag and all but trampled Oakwood's chief deputy rushing out the door.

Maggie picked up the packet of baby wipes her friend had left, and tried to slip away, too. The hand on her arm wasn't exactly a command to *halt,* but Maggie skidded to a stop inside the door all the same.

She should tell Angie what was going on. But Claire would never trust her again if she did.

"What's up?" Angie's voice was friendly but firm, which was a pretty good description of the woman herself.

For a cop, Angie got along great with the kids at the center—she and Uncle Tony, both. They'd become a great team, spending most of their off-duty afternoons coordinating cool activities. They didn't talk down to anyone, either. They treated teens like grown-ups. Like friends.

No matter who you were, you were okay with them, no questions asked. And one smart-mouthed kid after another in the county had started to trust them. Except Claire, who didn't trust anybody but Maggie.

"Nothing's up." Her stomach tightened at the lie.

"I know you two are friends." Angie looked at Maggie, as honest and straight-shooting as ever, even in her everyday khakis and a knit golf shirt. Today's shirt was the same cool green color as her eyes. "But

Claire's been hanging with a pretty rough crowd lately. If she's in some kind of trouble—"

"Claire's fine." Maggie held her breath against the urge to blurt out what she knew about Sam Walker. She ducked her head. "I...I've got to get home and help my uncle Tony with my parents' going-away thing. I...I'll see you later."

She made a quick escape, leaving Angie no chance for more questions. As she jogged toward the side door her friend had most likely left through, she thought of that night's family dinner and couldn't help but smile.

Her parents were leaving for New York in the morning, to scout places for the three of them to live in the fall. Maggie was staying behind this trip, fin-ishing summer school and the two classes she needed to graduate. She'd missed tons of school last year. The liver-donor surgery that had saved her mom's life had taken months to recover from.

Two more classes and her future was ahead of her. The kind of future Claire would never have if she kept hooking up with losers like Sam.

Outside, there was no sign of Claire or the boys they'd been hiding from. Boys, including Garret Henderson, who hung with Sam Walker almost every afternoon—doing what, Maggie could only guess.

What if telling Angie tonight was the right thing?

What if it was the only way to keep Sam from hurting Claire and the rest of the kids in town more than he already had?

Maggie shook off the what-ifs and headed home. She wanted to go after her friend. She wanted to go back and spill her guts to Angie. She wanted to fill her parents in on everything, and help shut Sam Walker and his drugs down for good. But she couldn't do any of it, not tonight.

She'd talk some sense into Claire in the morning. After her parents left for the airport, she'd head over and confront Sam himself if she had to.

Whatever it took to get her friend out of that apartment.

ANGIE WATCHED Maggie hightail it through the side door of the youth center as if the girl's low-rise jeans were on fire. Seeing her running scared was a shock.

Maggie was a Rivers through and through. Brown hair, intelligent brown eyes and a heart of gold. And a Rivers didn't run. From anything. In fact, they'd fight to the death—particularly to protect the people they cared about. And Maggie and Claire Morton had been as thick as thieves from the moment they'd met six months ago, when Maggie had tagged along during one of her uncle's volunteer nights at the center.

It had been an odd match, the sheriff's kid and a runaway who'd zeroed in on the toughest badass in town, gotten herself knocked up, and then moved herself and the baby in with Sam Walker for good measure. But Maggie had seen something in Claire worth saving, and that had been the end of her parents trying to talk her out of hanging with the girl every afternoon.

Something was up. Angie could smell it. But was she sure enough to make a stink about it, when her ability to work with the kids around here hinged on not interfering in their life choices unless it was an emergency?

The teens at the center were practically her surrogate children. She'd accepted the reality years ago that she couldn't have kids of her own. She'd dealt with the devastating impact that news had had on her dreams, and her never-to-be marriage to Freddie. Then she'd gone out and found a way to fill her life with kids regardless. Over the last few years, her volunteer work at the center and her career had become her salvation.

The teens here needed her, and she needed them. Her goal, the goal of all the volunteers who gave their time here, many of them sheriff's deputies like herself, was to keep the often at-risk kids coming back. Kids from broken or dual-income homes, where parental control was either scarce or nonexistent. Rural families that often didn't or couldn't provide the kind of supervision restless teenagers needed. She was a big sister here, a confidante who listened and helped any way she could, while doing everyday things like playing a friendly game of Ping-Pong or basketball.

Angie gritted her teeth against the memory of her last game of hoops with Travis Reynolds. She'd let Travis down by not getting rid of the crap someone had sold him. And now Claire Morton was acting nervous. And big-city-smart Maggie Rivers looked more worried than Angie had ever seen her. It didn't take a decade in law enforcement to guess what the problem was.

Baby Max's father was bad news. There were rumors Sam Walker was into Oakwood's crystal meth trade up to his eyeballs. The department had no proof. Yet. But he'd been working his way to the top of their suspects list ever since their first meth collar eight months ago. And the chance that Maggie had gotten herself involved in the drugs overtaking their county like cancer landed a knot dead center in Angie's stomach.

She couldn't let this slide.

Maggie's parents were leaving in the morning, and they'd been planning tonight's family dinner all week. With as little information as Angie had, she wasn't stirring up trouble their last evening in town. But once tomorrow's shift was over, Maggie Rivers had some questions to answer. Which would leave Angie talking to Tony if there was any truth to her suspicions.

Damn.

The man was the last person she should be spending her off-duty time talking to. She couldn't get it out of her head, the confused, almost disappointed look on his face when she'd pulled away from him at the Eight Ball.

Tony wore *unattached* like some kind of shield—exactly why she'd felt so safe spending time with him, talking about things she never talked about with anyone. And she'd listened to his stuff, too. The way a good friend does—hanging out, and listening and trying to understand.

Not to mention the creepy fact that once, like a million years ago in high school, she'd actually had a crush on the man's older brother.

They were friends. That was all. Just good friends.

Then Tony had pulled her into that kiss, and—

"There you are, Chief." The mayor's booming voice from the other end of the hall yanked her away from her memories.

The board meeting.

Before stepping into the restroom, she'd been

headed for the center's trustees meeting. She'd already been running late for their discussion about how the town's civic leaders could help deter the rising drug problem. A quick check of her watch confirmed that she'd now missed the entire meeting.

But instead of being angry, the mayor walked her way with a cheerful gait, his ever-present press gaggle in tow. He never missed an opportunity to corner her into face time with the local reporters. They were her mouthpiece to the community, he insisted. A powerful weapon in her bid for election, not to mention his determination to preserve his winning image now that he was publicly supporting her.

He shook her hand. His politician's smile played for their audience.

"I wasn't sure you were going to make it tonight." He turned slightly so the cameras caught his good side.

And she almost hadn't, even though it was one of her regular afternoons to volunteer. The mayor's blatant promotion of her candidacy chafed many of the deputies the wrong way, including her. His recent interest in the department didn't extend to talking the council into hiring more officers, or upgrading their facilities and equipment to help them better protect the county's citizens. All flash and no substance, Henderson was as supportive as it took to help himself and his own upcoming bid for reelection.

But she'd agreed to attend the board meeting, and this time she'd even agreed to the press. She'd do whatever it took to better educate people about the drug problem brewing in their backyards: local leaders, parents and anyone else who'd listen. The town had to band together to find a solution.

"Mr. Mayor." She smiled blandly into the glare of flashbulbs. "I'm willing to do anything for the kids, you know that."

"I've just come from meeting with the center's board of trustees, as you know," he said, more for the reporters than her. He nodded as Oliver Wilmington joined them. The old man walked painfully slowly these days, leaning heavily on the cane he'd relied on since recovering from last year's stroke. "And they're very impressed with your department's efforts in drug prevention, as well as your personal plans for the future, should you be elected sheriff. You know the chairman of the center's board, don't you?"

"Mr. Wilmington." She shook hands with Maggie Rivers's great-grandfather. Another flurry of flashbulbs temporarily blinded her. "The department is always happy to have the support of our local leaders."

"Actually," the elderly gentleman said, "I'm not entirely convinced either you or your department is up for this task. Not after that unfortunate boy's death this morning."

Angie nodded thoughtfully. Inside she cringed. Old Man Wilmington had never hidden his skepticism of her ability to make a good sheriff. Now everyone in town would be reading about it in tomorrow's paper.

"I—" she started.

"The chief's the man for the job." Mayor Henderson's hearty pat on the back, his forced enthusiasm in front of the two reporters hastily recording every word being said, grated almost as much as his insistence in repeating her title over and over again. As if anyone in town could forget that the only woman on the force was in charge of the nine men serving with her. "Putting this scum threatening Oakwood's teens and citizens behind bars is the cornerstone of Officer Carter's platform."

"Is that how you see it, Chief?" Cal Grossman, the *Oakwood Star*'s combination roving reporter and editorial chief, chimed in. His weekly spotlights on the ups and downs of her unopposed sheriff's *race* had become a local must-read. "That your run for the top spot hinges on stopping the increase in drug-related crime in the area?"

"Not to mention the gangs," Oliver Wilmington added. "What are you going to do about the gangs running amok through this historic town? Shootings, overdoses, graffiti scarring some of our most beloved buildings. It's appalling how little control the sheriff's department seems to have over any of it."

Angie looked from one man to another, feeling oddly like a reality-TV contestant who'd been set up to fail, meanwhile everyone was glued to his seat watching her squirm. Well, they'd have to look somewhere else for their entertainment today.

"Our department is totally committed, as I am, to handling all of these problems, gentlemen." She gave Wilmington a firm smile. "But my bid for sheriff couldn't be further from the point here. Our current sheriff and each of the deputies on this county's payroll have the same goal—protecting our citizens. Most importantly, our children."

"Like my son, Garret, here." The mayor all but dragged the eighteen-year-old from the fringes of the impromptu press conference. "Our focus has to stay on keeping these kids safe and out of trouble. And that's right up Chief Carter's alley. Why, she volunteers no fewer than ten hours each week to mentor the teens who come to this center. Personal time she could be spending any ol' way she wants. And she chooses to be here, working with kids who need the kind of guidance she—"

Angie tuned out the mayor's prattle and studied Garret Henderson instead. The boy wasn't exactly tops on her list of trouble-shy kids. She'd caught him hanging around Sam Walker and a few other miscreants a little too often lately. A couple of times, she'd found herself wondering if the kid wasn't strung out on something. Garret stood stiffly beside his dad. Silent—she'd like to think because of his grief over Travis Reynolds's death. Or maybe he tolerated being used as a prop in his father's political exploits even less gracefully than Angie did.

"If you'll excuse me." She left behind the scene threatening to turn her stomach.

"But, Chief Carter," Cal called after her. "Do you have any comment on your election hinging on how well you handle the drug problem, especially now that Sheriff Rivers is on extended leave?"

"No," was all she'd let herself say.

Sick of the mayor's tactics. Sick of talking about the sheriff's race—in which she was the sole candidate, but if a majority of the citizens didn't cast their vote, the city council would be given the duty of appointing an interim sheriff once Eric left in the fall. Sick to death that kids were dying, yet the election was all anyone, including herself, could think about most days, she headed out the front door of the youth center.

Exactly when had she started dreading the thought of campaigning for the job she'd hitched her future to? And how was it possible she longed to keep walking until she reached the Rivers place, so she could talk through her second thoughts about her career—not with her boss, but with his kid brother?

Not going to happen.

She'd decided to wait until morning to follow up with Maggie. She wouldn't interrupt their family's celebration for anything. Especially to talk with Tony.

But the man managed to see her. The *real* her buried beneath the competent cop. He didn't try to fix things she didn't want fixed, her family's favorite pastime when she let the doubt and fear slip free.

Tony would find a way to understand. He'd sit and listen to the confusion rolling around inside her head. The swamping guilt over Travis's death. Her wishy-washy angst about the election. Maybe he'd even find a way to make her laugh.

Actually, it didn't seem to matter what Tony did. It would be good to see him again. More than good. It would make the otherwise hopeless night ahead bearable.

Wonderful.

Why did Tony Rivers have to be exactly what she needed most, just when she'd promised herself she'd steer clear of the man?

CHAPTER THREE

"MAGGIE, YOU'VE GOTTA GO," Claire said the next morning. She cracked the door open a little wider. "Who knows when Sam'll be back. He's already in a bad mood."

"I'm not leaving without you, Claire." Maggie put her hand on the door to keep her friend from shutting it in her face. No way was she giving up this easily. "Where's Max?"

"In his crib. Sleeping, thank God. I'm trying to clean while I've got a few minutes."

"'Cause Sam's too lazy to pick up after himself?"

"No, because he was hopping mad about the place when he left." Claire wiped eyes that looked swollen from crying. "I don't want to deal with him coming back and getting mad all over again. It scares Max so bad, all that yelling."

"Let me in." Maggie reached inside and squeezed her friend's hand. "Let me help clean. You look dead tired."

With shaking fingers, Claire slid the chain back and swung the door wide. *Tired* wasn't the right word. It looked as if she hadn't slept at all last night. And she hadn't been exaggerating about the apartment. Dirty clothes, dishes and baby things were strewn everywhere.

"Ew." Maggie pried a container of Chinese takeout from where it had spilled and adhered to the coffee table.

"I don't know how I could let everything get so filthy." Claire took the mess from Maggie and tossed it into the unlined wicker trash can in the corner. "I'm just—"

"You're just a new mom with no help around here, who's trying to take care of a baby entirely on your own. Where's this family of Sam's? Why hasn't his mother pitched in, if things are this bad?"

"Sam won't ask Betty for help. His family never comes here. We always go to their farm out near Pineview. Once I get things under control, we'll be fine." Claire picked up a pile of soiled laundry. Tripping over a stuffed bunny, she caught herself on the end table beside the couch and toppled a shoe box to the floor. It landed on its side. A revolver rolled out.

"Oh my God." Claire reached for the gun.

"Don't touch it!" Maggie pulled her away. "Who knows what it's been used for."

"What?" Fear filled her friend's hoarse whisper.

"You said Sam and those guys were talking about a drive-by shooting. What if—"

"No." Claire sat on the couch, shaking her head slowly. "I can't believe that Sam—"

"Of course you believe it!" Keeping quiet about Sam's connection to Oakwood's drug problem had tortured Maggie all through her parent's send-off dinner, into the night, and right up until she'd kissed her mom and dad goodbye that morning. Then she'd all but run from her uncle's good-buddy suggestion that they spend the day together. "What I can't figure out is *how* you can believe it, and still be here with your baby."

"Exactly where am I supposed to go, with no money and no way of getting any, except from Sam and his family?"

"Call your parents." Maggie sat and put an arm around her friend. Claire was out of time and easy options. "You said they live somewhere near Williamsburg. That's not so far way. I'm sure if they knew—"

"My parents are hundreds of miles from here, and don't be so sure they'd help. When I left, they were lecturing me about being a high-school dropout. Add an unwed mother to the bargain, and—"

"They'll want you back. And they'll want Max, too, once they have a chance to know him. And you can stay with me until you reach them."

"What about when Sam finds out? His mom won't let me take Max—"

"No one has to know you're at my house. My parents are on their way to New York."

Maggie already missed her parents, and they would be back in a few weeks. Claire hadn't seen her family in almost two years. She must be dying inside.

"It's the weekend," Maggie pressed. "We'll lie low and figure this out together. Sam'll think you skipped town or something."

Claire was shaking her head again. She seemed to have run out of arguments. Maggie slipped the gun back inside the shoe box by nudging it with the lid. Then using the toe of her sneaker, she slid the whole thing as far away as she could.

"It's not safe here. My uncle will help you keep Max away from Sam and his family for a few days, and by Monday you'll be on your way to Virginia."

Maggie heard herself make the promise and prayed Tony would play along. It wasn't like she and her uncle were überclose or anything. He was fun to hang out with, but serious stuff wasn't his style. But after she showed up with Claire, what choice would he have? Maggie wasn't taking no for an answer, from him or her friend.

"Once you're back with your parents, they'll work

out how to legally keep Max with you and away from the Walkers."

And you can help my dad and his deputies nail Sam's ass to the wall.

"I...I'd have to pack up all of Max's stuff. I...I don't know..."

"I'll help." Maggie pulled her friend to her feet and half shoved her into the other room. Sam might come back at any minute. "Just bring whatever Max'll need for the next couple of days. You can borrow some of my clothes, and your parents will help you with the rest once you get to Virginia."

A peek inside the portable crib between the bed and the wall confirmed that Max was sleeping soundly. From the mess in the closet, Claire produced an oversize duffel that Maggie helped her fill with diapers, baby clothes and the tiny toys Max chewed on almost constantly, now that he was teething.

"What about food?" Maggie couldn't zip the overflowing bag, so she left it gaping open. "Do you need anything we can't pick up at the grocery?"

"I'm still nursing mostly." Claire set aside the extra blanket she'd taken from the playpen and headed for the bedroom door. "There's half a box of rice cereal in the kitchen, and a few bottles of the fruit I've been trying to get him to eat—"

The front door swung open with a thump, cutting

Claire off. Maggie grabbed her friend's arm and pulled her back into the room. Together, they tiptoed to the corner by the crib. Claire held her finger to her lips, an unnecessary bid for silence.

"Damn, man, you weren't kidding about this place," an unfamiliar male voice said. "It smells like baby poop in here."

"It's the damn diaper pail in the bathroom," Sam groused in his distinctive Southern drawl. "Claire?" he called.

The girls froze, glancing nervously to where Max was snoozing the morning away.

"Thank God," Sam said. "She must have taken the brat somewhere."

"You as a daddy," the other man joked. "I never thought you were stupid enough to get a piece of white trash like Claire Morton pregnant."

"Yeah?" Sam's chuckle was a menacing thing. Beside Maggie, Claire was shaking in her sandals. "I guess it's about as stupid as you nailing Digger Hudson last month, in broad daylight a block from the youth center. Now the cops are crawling all over the place. It's cutting into my business."

"Is that why you brought me down here, to bust my hump about the drive-by? Man, that was weeks ago. I just ran your shit halfway to Memphis and back, and I dumped a small fortune in your lap. Don't that count for nothin'? Digger was skimming half your take. You told me to take care of him."

"Quietly, Marcus. I told you to take care of him real quiet-like. Now the town's in even more of an uproar."

"So what? You've got a new dealer for Digger's territory, and he's doing more business than you can handle. The kids around here are buying the stuff like it's candy. You can't make it fast enough. Besides, the mayor and his hired guns ain't got nothin', or they'd have come looking for me by now. You're untouchable."

"They may have nothing yet, but I had to move another lab this morning. And one of my runners almost got nabbed at the bus station on his way to a dealer in Macon. The money in Atlanta is getting edgy. I live and die by my reputation. I can't afford to be seen as high risk. Too much local interference, and I'm out. There are other towns, with less cops and less complications. The people who back me don't want to deal with that kind of heat. So what I've *got,* is a great big pain in my ass, with your name written all over it."

"Now wait a minute—"

"No, you wait! You're out, Marcus. You ain't goin' to up and decide to be stupid again, not in my town. Get the hell out of Oakwood, and don't let me catch you around here again."

"You can't—"

"I can do whatever the hell I want," Sam bellowed. "And you ain't got jack to say about it. Get the hell out of my apartment, and don't make the mistake of lying low anywhere around here. My people are everywhere. People a whole lot more loyal to me than they are to you. There's no place for you to hide."

"You son of a bitch," the other man growled, then from the sound of the scuffling and the colorful curses that followed, he took a swing at Sam.

Flying furniture rattled the wall separating the two rooms. Male grunts accompanied the sound of fists connecting with numerous body parts. Maggie held her breath. Her friend's wild eyes filled with tears.

Too late was all Maggie could think. Why hadn't she forced Claire to come home with her last night? Max was going to wake up any minute, then Sam and this Marcus guy were going to know Maggie and Claire were there and had overheard everything.

She edged to the crib and lifted the sleeping baby and his cocoon of bedding to her shoulder. She covered his head with a blanket to better drown out the racket from the next room.

"You bastard," someone said in a strangled voice, followed by more fighting.

Then an ear-piercing explosion rocketed through the apartment, followed almost instantly by another.

Claire and Maggie dropped to the floor in one motion, cowering together while Maggie jostled a squirming Max.

Oh my God, they were shooting at each other!

Then the air that Maggie couldn't seem to breathe rang with silence.

Had they left?

The sound of feet shuffling told her that at least one of the guys was still there. Then the front door banged open, followed by more silence.

Max began making puppylike sounds. Maggie cuddled him closer, trying to keep him quiet until they were certain they were alone. An eternity passed before she dared a glance at her friend. Claire was leaning against the wall still, looking toward the closet, her chest heaving up and down in shock at what had happened.

"Claire," Maggie whispered. "Do you think they're gone?"

When her friend didn't respond, Maggie risked nudging her with her shoulder, more than a little worried that any second Claire would start shrieking. But her friend's chin dropped to her chest instead. Her upper body slowly slid sideways until she was lying on the floor. Blood smeared the wall behind her.

"Oh my God!" Maggie whispered, panic hammering through her. She jerked a glance toward the open closet door, zeroing in on the hole where a bullet had torn through the wall and then slammed into her friend. "Claire!"

Maggie couldn't manage anything louder than a whisper, even though she was freaking out inside. It was all she could do not to drop the whimpering baby in her arms as she watched blood spread like tie-dye across her friend's Atlanta Braves T-shirt.

Claire's eyes were open. Her chest was still moving as she tried to take in air. But each breath was a struggling wheeze. Maggie scrambled closer.

"Claire, hold on." She reached a tentative hand to touch her friend's chalk-white cheek. The skin beneath her fingers was cold. Too cold. "I'm calling 911."

"No…" Claire rasped before Maggie could move away. "N-No police. Get… Get Max out of here."

"What are you talking about?" Maggie's eyes filled at the weakness in her friend's voice. "I'm getting you to the hospital."

"No…" An attempt at a cough followed, then bright red blood dribbled from the corner of Claire's mouth. "Get Max out first. Then call. I'll be… fine…" More coughing cut her words off, each ugly sound weaker than the last. "Get Max out of here…. To my parents…like you promised."

Maggie looked from her friend to the bright blue eyes of the squirming infant in her arms.

"Of course I'll make sure he gets to Virginia," she heard herself promising.

Max's face scrunched as he revved up to start wailing. She rocked him harder, helpless to do anything else.

She'd never felt helpless before in her life.

"Please!" Claire's hand clamped on Maggie's arm with surprising strength. "Go… Now. What if they come back? Max can't be here…. Not… Not safe… Sam can't know you were here. You… You promised to help. Protect him for me, Maggie. Take care of Max…."

Claire's hand slid to the ground. Her eyes rolled backward in a sickening glide, until her lids dropped shut.

"Claire?" Maggie knelt and felt her friend's chest, which was thankfully still rising and falling. She pulled her hand away, only to stare at the crimson staining it. Her friend's blood. She choked on another scream. "Claire, wake up! Claire?"

Too late, her mind chanted.

She could have stopped this last night, but now it was too late.

"Oh, God!"

Move, Maggie Rivers.

She staggered to her feet. Max's cry sent her heart rate spiraling even higher. She returned him to his makeshift crib, his bottom hitting the pad with a squishy-diaper thud. Then she was racing through the door to find the phone in the den.

She tripped over something and landed hard on her hands and knees. Preparing to push back to her feet, she focused on the hand barely two inches from her nose. A hand grasping a gun.

In a crazy kind of slow motion she couldn't stop, Maggie's gaze trailed up the arm attached to the hand, finally coming to rest on the face of a man she didn't know. A face covered with a sickening amount of blood.

Her screams joined Max's.

She raced to the phone and dialed. What seemed like hours passed and the 911 operator still hadn't picked up.

Why wouldn't they pick up!

"911 Emergency," a calm, feminine voice finally answered.

"Please," Maggie begged through her chattering teeth. "Please... People have been shot. S-Send an ambulance."

She recited the apartment's location as she glanced back to the bedroom. The baby's cries had reached ear-splitting decibels.

"And the names of the victims?" the operator asked.

"What?" Maggie stared at the clearly dead stranger on the living room's shabby beige carpet.

Marcus.

Sam had called him Marcus, then he'd shot him. And one of the men had shot Claire.

"The victims," the woman prompted. "I need their names."

Get Max out of here... Not safe...Sam can't know you were here...

"Their names?" Maggie repeated.

"Yes, names." Suspicion crept into the woman's voice. "Why don't we start with yours. Is that your baby I hear crying?"

Protect him for me, Maggie.... Get Max out of here.... To my parents...like you promised.

"Miss? The paramedics are on their way. Please give me your name. How did the shootings occur?"

Maggie slammed the phone onto its receiver. Fought not to run screaming out of the apartment. She had to stay and make sure Claire was okay. She should wait for her dad's deputies to get there.

But if she did, they'd take Max away for sure.

Protect him for me, Maggie....

She stumbled to the bedroom and found Claire still unconscious, though she was breathing. Baby Max was beside himself, demanding to be picked up. She grabbed him and knelt beside her friend.

"Claire, the ambulance is on its way." Maggie jiggled the baby, scared out of her mind, but trying not to sound it. "Claire, can you hear me?"

No response came, only Max's whimpers.

God, please don't let my friend die.

This was all her fault. None of this would have happened if she'd talked to Angie, or her parents or somebody yesterday.

Get Max out of here....

She didn't dare. Running with the baby was stupid. But she'd promised.... Once the paramedics and her dad's deputies got there, would they really turn Max over to his local family?

Sam's family.

Tears streaming down her face, she pulled herself together and up off the floor. Forget how sick she felt. Forget how much she wanted to hold her friend close and start sobbing right along with the baby.

Don't be a coward, Maggie.

Don't just stand there. Move!

Shaking, she kissed Claire's forehead and said another quick prayer she was terrified was too little, too late. Then she did the scariest thing she'd ever done in her life.

She ran.

CHAPTER FOUR

SPENDING HIS SATURDAY OFF doing what he thought any self-respecting, stand-in parent should be doing, Tony pulled a fresh batch of laundry from the dryer. With classic rock blaring from the radio on the shelf behind the washer, he breathed in the scent of detergent and home, and shoved aside thoughts of his family's imminent move to New York.

Last night's dinner had been great.

It was all great.

So put Eric's move out of your mind, man. It's a done deal.

Except his mind didn't clear as Billy Joel sang about a sweet girl named Virginia, as much as it shifted to thoughts of a certain chief deputy.

The softness of her lips. The fact that he felt like he belonged wherever they were, every time they were alone. The curves he'd discovered beneath her unisex clothes, filling his hands—

The side door off the kitchen crashed open.

His niece was home from wherever she'd disappeared to an hour ago. When she sped upstairs without saying hello, he dropped the towels back into the dryer and headed after her. Billy crooned that only the good died young.

Maybe he and Maggie could grab burgers and shakes for lunch. Maybe they could hang out for the rest of the day. The world would be fine again, as soon as he got his head out of his butt and stopped obsessing about things he couldn't change. Not to mention a woman he was nuts to want in the first place.

"Mags?" He took the steps two at time. "What's up?"

The only response was muffled shuffling from the direction of his niece's room. Then her door slammed shut in a very un-Maggie way.

In three long strides, he was knocking.

"Maggie, you okay?" His hand hovered over the doorknob.

A mewling sound that resembled a kitten's cry came from the other side of the door. When it turned into a full-fledged wail that most definitely wasn't feline, he tried the knob.

It was locked.

No one locked doors around here.

"Maggie, what's going on?"

"I… Everything's fine." Her voice shook with

each word, what he could hear of it over the racket of an increasingly upset baby. "Um—"

"Maggie, open the door." Tony gave up knocking and started pounding, fun afternoon plans evaporating.

He'd heard his totally together niece sound this scared only one other time. Last year, when he'd learned of her mother's life-threatening liver condition. Maggie and Eric hadn't been able to talk Carrinne into letting Maggie donate a portion of her liver to replace her mom's, and it had looked for a short time like they might lose his sister-in-law. Maggie had been out-of-control angry, terrified as she'd pleaded with Carrinne to change her mind.

The same emotion owned her voice now. Something was seriously wrong.

As if the hysterical baby wasn't clue enough.

"Open this door now, Maggie, or I swear, I'll break it down!"

Like his niece needed a cop barreling through her door.

Sheesh, tone it down, man.

He'd had the next few weeks planned so perfectly. He was a kick-ass uncle. Maggie loved hanging out with him. Suddenly, the only ass he wanted to kick was his brother's, for not being there to head this off.

"Come on, Mags," Tony cajoled. "Whatever it

is, I can help. And if I can't, we'll call your folks, and they'll—"

"No!" The lock turned and the door was yanked open, revealing the shocking sight of his niece, her face drained of color, holding a squalling infant. Her friend's baby, if Tony didn't miss his guess.

"Why do you have Max?" he asked. "Is Claire—"

He'd been about to say *okay,* when the splashes of color marring the front of Maggie's white T-shirt hit home.

"Oh my God, you're bleeding," he managed to say as the floor sank beneath him.

He backed her unresisting body toward the bed and gently pushed her and the baby down. Without taking his hand off Maggie's shoulder, he grabbed the portable phone from a nearby table. He misdialed three times.

"Lie down. Don't move. I'll have an ambulance here in a few min—"

"No!" Maggie whipped the phone out of his hand and jumped to her feet. Terminating the call, she threw the receiver across the room. Life sparked back into her eyes. A touch of color warmed her cheeks. "I'm fine. It's not my blood. It's… It's… I'm fine."

"Whose blood is it, Maggie?" She couldn't have moved so quickly if she were seriously injured. What he'd thought was fresh blood was actually dried. His panic yielded to a flurry of questions. "What the hell's going on? Where's Claire? Why do you have Max?"

"I…I was…" Tears filled her eyes. That strong chin that was so much like his and his brother's began to wobble. "Please, Tony. You have to help me. Claire's hurt…. And she made me promise to get Max to her parents in Virginia…. I can't let Sam's family have him…. And the…there was this guy on the floor, and…and I think he's dead…. He…Sam shot him, and he could have come back at any minute, so I called the ambulance and…and then I ran…."

She was pacing with the crying baby now—his nineteen-year-old niece, saying things straight out of his nightmares. Tony could only stare in silence as he processed the jumbled images her words painted. Then she stopped and brought the hand not holding Max to her mouth.

"Tony, she's hurt so bad. Claire… They shot her…."

Rousing himself into motion, he made Maggie sit on the edge of the bed again. Max's wails were winding down, thank the heavens above. His tiny head was nestled in the crook of her neck as he whimpered. Tony left the baby there, even though his training told him Maggie should be lying down until some of her shock wore off.

Her shock?

Holy hell. He pulled her and the baby into a fierce hug, tamping down the urge to fire another string of questions his niece was in no shape to answer.

She was safe. She was okay. And by God, he was going to keep her that way.

"Don't worry. I'm not going to let anything happen to you or Max," he promised.

As a matter of fact, he wasn't letting her out of his sight, at least not until he got his brother back here to sort this out. He left the bed long enough to retrieve the phone from the corner.

"I'm calling Angie. She's on duty this morning, and she'll—"

"No!" Maggie was up again, shaking until her teeth chattered. She pointed a determined finger at him. "Call anyone, and I swear I'm out of here. No one can know I have Max. No one can know we were there. If you call Angie, she'll have to turn the baby over to someone, most likely Sam's family, and I promised Claire…" Maggie's face crumpled at the mention of her friend. "I promised her I wouldn't let that happen. Please, Tony. Please don't call Angie. You said you'd help me. Please…"

Tony looked from the receiver to Maggie. She was gumption and brains at their brightest. And like her mother, she didn't know how to fall apart. But at the moment, the niece who'd laid claim to his supposedly shallow heart looked every bit the vulnerable teenager she still was.

She was terrified. And though he couldn't follow half of what she'd said, he understood enough to be scared for both her and her friend. Maggie had witnessed a shooting at the very least. It sounded like two people were injured, if not dead. At Sam Walker's hand?

"I have to call this in, Maggie. You're in danger, and Claire might be seriously hurt—"

"No!" She made a ridiculous attempt to take the phone away from him again. "I called 911 before I left. Angie or someone else is already there by now. Please, help me get Max away from Oakwood."

"Away to where? Tell me what's going—"

The doorbell's chime cut him off.

Maggie flinched, glancing nervously over her shoulder then back at Tony.

"Ignore it," he groused. But the bell rang again for a longer stretch. "Damn it, who—"

She grabbed his arm. "No one can know Max is here."

"It's not that simple, Maggie!"

More ringing sounded, over and over this time. The baby started fussing, another tantrum threatening.

"Ah, hell." Tony ran a hand through his hair, shoved the phone at his niece and pointed to the bed.

"Park your butt there, and don't even think about moving it until I get back."

He trudged toward the stairs.

"Tony, you won't—"

"Sit!" he said, louder than he'd intended.

But it got the desired effect. His niece swallowed, then she sank to the edge of the bed. Her silence, the sadness and fear clinging to her as clearly as the baby in her arms, made it almost impossible for him to walk away. But whoever was at the door showed no sign of letting up.

The trek down the stairs didn't leave him nearly enough time to piece together Maggie's scraps of information. Insistent knocking had replaced the bell by the time he yanked the weathered front door open.

"Angie." He blinked as the very person he'd been determined to call materialized on his welcome mat.

Relief flooded him at the sight of her sweet face. Then her harried expression, the way she gazed over his shoulder, hit him upside the head with the reality of what must have brought her there.

"Is Maggie home?" she asked at the same moment that the baby squealed upstairs. "There's been an incident with her friend Claire."

CHAPTER FIVE

PLEASE LET MAGGIE BE TUCKED safely in bed.

Angie hadn't stopped repeating the simple plea the entire drive over. Dressed for the job, she'd been on her way in for duty when the traffic from the 911 call had come over her receiver. Then her cell phone had begun ringing nonstop.

She'd had two options. Head to the scene through the early morning fog, when there were already deputies en route. Or do what she should have done last night—follow her hunch that Maggie Rivers and Claire Morton were flirting with trouble, and pay a visit to the Rivers house.

Oakwood had lost two teens in less than twenty-four hours. First Travis Reynolds. Now Claire.

Knowing she might have been able to stop this latest tragedy, Angie fought a wave of nausea. If only she'd pushed the girls for more information yesterday. If only she hadn't let the mayor drag her into another press conference, or let the uncomfortable crap between her and Tony help make waiting until morning sound like a smart choice.

Now, with the gruesome details coming in fast from the homicide scene, she couldn't bring herself to look the man in the eye.

Tell me Maggie's been home safe and sound all morning.

Please.

Another distant wail came from inside the house, just like the first one. It sounded like—

A baby?

Then it dawned that Tony hadn't said a word. He hadn't asked her in. In fact, he was staring straight through her. A rush of adrenaline prickled the skin at the back of her neck.

"Is Maggie here?" She grasped for a professional tone, shifting into "cop-mode," as her sister, Lissa, called it. A skill Angie had never before used on a friend.

Do your job. For heaven's sake, do the damn job before someone else gets hurt!

"Um—" Tony's smile was strained. "I'm not sure."

"I'm here on department business. I need to talk with her." Angie was already stepping forward.

"No!"

He gripped the door and placed his six-foot-and-more frame between her and entry into the house.

"I mean, *no*." The word came out softer the second time, but no less determined. "Maggie's not here."

"You said you weren't sure—"

"I meant I haven't seen her since Eric and Carrinne headed for the airport after breakfast. As far as I know, I'm the only one home."

A muffled crash contradicted him. When he half turned to look behind him, a firm forearm to his chest and a shove cleared enough space for Angie to slip by.

"Hey!" He grabbed her arm. "I said—"

"Yeah, Maggie's not here. Got it."

He was lying. What an odd thing, for something like that to hurt like hell in the midst of everything else. She scanned the comfortably lived-in family room, looking beyond to the hallway stairs.

"Was that a baby I heard?"

"No, it's the TV in the kitchen. I told you—"

"Right. You're here alone." Angie slipped out of his grasp, which never would have happened if *Mr. Easy Does It* hadn't been so obviously undone.

A thud echoed from the direction of the kitchen. She made a beeline for the sound. Burst into the room to find the sink a mess, the stove covered with the remains of breakfast, and everything else looking exactly as it should on a lazy Saturday morning.

Except the TV wasn't on, as Tony had said, and whoever or whatever had made the noise they'd heard was nowhere to be found. Angie looked from him, to the side door she could see through the laundry room, then back.

"You need to leave," said the man who two nights ago had begged her not to walk away. His easygoing act was gone, replaced by the steely resolve she'd always known lurked beneath.

"I *need* to make sure Maggie's okay. Then I need to speak with her."

"I told you, she's not—"

"Claire Morton's dead."

Angie watched Tony's complexion blanch from unnaturally pale to totally white.

She knew exactly how he felt.

"Buddy Tyler and Martin Rhodes responded to a 911 from her boyfriend's apartment a half hour ago. There was another body at the scene besides Claire, but it's not the girl's boyfriend. Yesterday afternoon, I stumbled across Maggie and Claire at the youth center. Claire was upset, but they clammed up as soon as they saw me. I need to ask Maggie if she knows anything about—"

"Claire's dead?" Tony sucked in a breath. Rocking back on his heels, he stared at the ceiling. "Holy shit."

"She was gone before Rhodes and Tyler got there." Angie's voice wavered. Doing the job was hell, when everything felt personal. "Along with one of the goons her boyfriend hangs around town with. We figure Sam for the shot that took out his buddy. As for who hit Claire… It looks like there may have been two guns fired at the scene. My first thought was that Maggie might know something. Maybe the girls were worried—"

"Wait a minute." She finally had Tony's undivided attention. "You thought something was wrong yesterday, but you're only getting around to coming by for a chat now!"

"I…I wasn't sure of anything…." Angie swallowed her excuse. Fought to breathe. "I thought it would be better to wait—"

"Until someone got killed?"

"Until this morning!" she snapped. She'd never forgive herself. "I had no idea Claire was into anything this serious."

"And now that you are, you're Johnny-on-the-spot? You have two bodies, so *regulations* say it's time to question my niece. And here you are, knocking on our door. Hey, if you hurry and call the mayor, the two of you might just make the midday news."

Everything inside Angie froze.

"The press is already circling Claire's apartment. I came here instead, because I'm worried." He couldn't really believe she'd put ambition, the election or anything else ahead of protecting Maggie. "I care about you and your family. I don't give a damn about making a splash on tomorrow's front page."

Tony started to sling another comeback. Then he blinked and some of the frost melted from those dark-as-sin eyes.

"I'm sorry," he said. "That was uncalled for."

She waved away the apology.

"*I'm* sorry. I know this is a terrible situation, and I wish I'd done more last night. But I have to talk with Maggie. Evidence at the scene is telling us Sam Walker is heavy into crystal meth. He may even be the local source we're gunning for. If Maggie knows anything, she has to make a statement. For her own protection, as well as to help us nail the bastard."

"Her protection?" Tony's incredulous smile was light-years from the charming grin that had melted her heart. "We have our second and third drug-related deaths in forty-eight hours. You think my niece is mixed-up in the middle of it. And you want her to make a formal statement, so the man responsible for all of it can turn his sights on her?" Tony picked up a dish towel and went to work on the pancake spatters decorating the stove. "Like I said. I haven't seen Maggie all morning. There's no one home but me."

"Is that right?" Angie was used to getting less than the truth when she confronted the family of witnesses and suspects. Tony lying to her shouldn't feel like a personal attack. But it did. "First, you treat me like a stranger and refuse to let me in. Then I hear a baby crying—which, coincidentally, so did the 911 dispatcher who took the call from Sam Walker's apartment. A young girl around Maggie's age was hysterical, and so was an infant in the background. But I guess I'm supposed to ignore the fact that you're acting like a man with something to hide, and take your word for it that you're here alone?"

"That's right."

From his first day out of the academy, Tony had been a fearless protector of the law. He was one of the best deputies Angie had ever worked with. His fast-and-loose act aside, protecting those who couldn't protect themselves was in his blood, just like his dad and his brother. Only now she was asking him to choose between the job and his family.

No shock who the winner was going to be.

Which made her the unwilling bad cop in this little melodrama.

"I'm sorry," she said. He'd never know how much. "But if Maggie was anywhere near that apartment this morning, she could be in a world of danger. I can't protect her if I don't know what's going on. And I can't not take her statement if she can help the department protect the rest of the town from what Sam Walker's doing."

Hating the job more than she ever thought she could, Angie turned and double-timed it up the stairs.

"Maggie," she called. Tony dogged her step for step. "It's Angie, honey. Don't be afraid. All I want to do is help. I know you're scared, but we need to talk. Is Max with you?"

She took a left at the upstairs landing.

"You're trespassing." Tony's growl had teeth as she walked through the open door to Maggie's room. "Angie—"

The absolute emptiness of the room silenced him. He was at the closet in an instant, peering in.

"Where did they go?" he demanded.

Instead of answering, Angie stepped to the bed. She fingered the softness of the single baby sock lying there, then she picked it up and turned back to Tony.

"Where did *who* go?"

TONY IGNORED ANGIE'S SARCASM and checked for Maggie's backpack where it always sat at the foot of the bed. Not only was the bag missing, but the cell phone and wallet he'd seen on the bedside table were also no-shows. The cordless phone he'd wrestled from his niece lay atop the twisted bedspread.

He grabbed it and pressed Redial to see if Maggie had called anyone.

The phone's display flashed a long-distance

number that he redialed. A high-pitched squeal heralded a prerecorded message telling him that the number had been disconnected. For more information, he could press 0.

He cut the connection and tossed the phone back onto the bed.

What the hell did he do now? Call his brother? Try to find Maggie first, because what could Eric do all the way from New York, anyway?

"Stop trying to handle this alone, Tony." Angie's gentle voice seeped through his confusion. "Talk to me. Let me in, so I can help."

He didn't dare. He couldn't talk to anyone until he knew more himself. Until he got his hands on his niece and called his brother.

Eric and Carrinne were going to freak.

He sat on the edge of the bed, dropping his head into his hands while he tried to sort out something in the vicinity of a game plan. Maggie had clearly heard his conversation with Angie and run. But run to where, and why? By now, she had to realize how much danger she was in.

God, she'd witnessed not one murder, but two. She'd overheard heaven only knew what, and she was wanted for questioning by the department.

But what had been his niece's number-one priority? Smuggling a baby out of town! And she'd slipped right through his fingers. The thought of Sam or one of his gang finding Maggie first, hurting her or the baby, would have taken Tony's knees out from under him if he hadn't already been sitting.

"Dispatch, this is Carter."

Angie was speaking into the com unit attached at the shoulder of her uniform. She turned up the volume on the receiver clipped to her belt. Static and a jumble of radio traffic filled the room.

"I need an update from the Walker apartment, and I need an APB out for Mag—"

Tony tore her hand away from the button that held the line open for her transmission.

"Don't," he pleaded. He tightened his grip on her fingers when she tried to pull away. "Give me a minute to think, damn it."

"Say again, Chief?" Marge, the on-duty dispatcher, responded. "I didn't get your APB."

A cop's instincts warred with the compassion in Angie's expression.

He knew the regs. Hell, if it weren't Maggie on the run, he'd be the one following the book to the letter. But they *were* talking about his niece. And Angie had come here first, because she was as worried as he was. His niece and his family had been her first concern.

Let me in.

Like he knew how.

"Please." He let her hand slide away. The impulse to reach for her again had him gritting his teeth. "If no one else suspects Maggie was at Claire's apartment, she's safe for now. Don't send someone to hunt her down. Not until we know for sure what we're dealing with."

"Do you know where she is?"

A quick shake of his head deepened the lines hugging her frown.

"Would you even tell me if you did?"

"Chief?" Marge prompted, saving him from answering.

He was interfering with police business. It could cost him his job. It could cost Angie more—a whole lot more than the rumors about their brief clinch at the Eight Ball. He'd told himself for two days now that he and this woman were no good for each other, ever since it had become impossible to keep memories of Angie corralled under the safe heading of Just Friends. Now he was asking her to put her future on the line.

But he had to find Maggie.

"Please," he said again, the word roughened by the thought of not getting to his niece in time. "Help me find Maggie, before anyone realizes she was at Claire's. The department will have all the answers you need once we do."

Angie's eyes locked onto his like green lasers, seeing through the bull he manufactured for the rest of the world, same as always. Understanding what he'd only recently begun to see in himself. How he always kept moving, no ties, nothing holding him to one person for too long. Not even to Maggie, who hadn't trusted him to stick by her this morning.

And if there was one thing Angie could relate to, it was choosing a life of loneliness; then living with the choice. That simple understanding had created an unexpected attraction between them. Two nights ago, as he'd fought off his panic at the thought of not seeing her outside of work anymore, he'd realized he craved their time together on a level far beyond physical. Around Angie, it was okay to be his mixed-up self. She was a safe place he hadn't known he needed until she'd walked away.

Now without her help, he couldn't keep Maggie safe.

"Hold off on the APB," Angie said into the com. "Get me an update from the Walker apartment as soon as you have something."

When another communication blasted through the room—Martin reporting in from the scene, wondering where the hell the medical examiner was—she turned the receiver's volume down to a dull buzz.

"So?" Her tone settled into all business. But her eyes softened. "Tell me what you know. And don't even think about lying to me again."

CHAPTER SIX

"PLEASE, NINA." MAGGIE JIGGLED Max higher on her shoulder. He'd been inconsolable since she'd thrown on clean clothes and run from her house. "I didn't know where else to go. I need a few things, then we'll be out of your hair."

"Give that baby to me before you drop him." Her great-grandfather's housekeeper all but dragged the squirming infant away.

Maggie, concerned Max's cries would echo through her great-grandfather's enormous mansion, hurried to shut the kitchen door that led to the rest of the house. Thankfully, Nina had been there when she'd sneaked in the back door.

"How long has it been since he's eaten?" the elderly woman asked.

"I... His mother..." Thinking of Claire lying motionless, her clothes stained in blood, made it impossible to finish.

Her cell phone rang and she fumbled to press the

off button, not even bothering to see who'd called. It could only be her uncle. Again.

"Where's his diaper bag?" Nina asked. "You don't have any of his things?"

Maggie shook her head. Words still wouldn't come.

She'd left the bag behind at Claire's, along with everything else they'd been packing, and she'd run from her uncle's before she'd had time to look for anything there. She had a little money in her backpack, but it wasn't like she could stop by the grocery to pick up baby stuff. Not if she wanted to keep the fact that she had Max a secret. From what she'd overheard at home, the sheriff's department would be looking for her soon, if they weren't already.

"Go get some milk from the fridge, and a Ziploc bag from the pantry," Nina glanced from the closed kitchen door back to Maggie, intelligent black eyes narrowing. "And while you're at it, suppose you tell me what's going on, and who this baby belongs to."

"My friend, Cla—" She swallowed Claire's name and headed for the pantry. The less Nina knew, the better. "His mother's in trouble, and she needs me to make sure he gets to her parents in Virginia."

"What about the baby's father?" Nina cuddled Max closer.

"He's… He…" Maggie fought back the tears. Fought to believe Claire was going to be okay. She set the half gallon of milk and box of baggies on the lace-covered kitchen table. "I can't let him know I have Max. I promised my friend I'd take care of her baby myself."

"On your own?" Nina stopped her soothing baby-rock. "Are you trying to tell me you're running off with this baby all on your own?"

"I…I just need to get him something to eat and some diapers." Maggie plastered on her version of her uncle's *everything's fine* smile. "Then we'll be all set."

"Is that right?" The housekeeper sounded less than convinced.

Maggie's mom had gone on and on about how Nina had been one of the few constants in her life. The Wilmington cook and housekeeper could always be counted on, her mom had said, for support and encouragement and wisdom. Right now, Maggie could do with a heaping dose of all three.

So why did you run from Tony?

Because Angie was there!

What choice had she had? Her call to Virginia information had resulted in a disconnected number for Claire's parents. And when she'd overheard Angie demanding to see her…

Nina was staring, as if Maggie had grown three heads or something. Then the woman nodded. Nothing more. Nothing dramatic. Then she accepted all Maggie had said, and all she hadn't, with an understanding squeeze of Maggie's shoulder. She handed Max back.

Opening one of the baggies and uncapping the milk, she poured a bit of the liquid into the bag, zipped it shut, and snipped a tiny hole in one of the bottom corners with a pair of kitchen shears. Placing her finger on the dripping corner, she held the bag up to Max.

"Let's dribble some of this into his mouth and see if he's interested. One night when Calvin and I were babysitting my niece's youngest, we ran out of bottles," the woman prattled on. No big deal. No big ugly monster standing right there in the room next to them. "This worked like a charm."

When the crying baby nestled in the crook of Maggie's arm gave a hiccup, and in the process managed to swallow some of the milk drooling over his lips and down his chin, his hands came up to grab at the bag. His rosebud mouth opened for more. Chuckling, Nina motioned for Maggie to take the bag.

"When they get hungry enough," Maggie's unlikely savior said, "they'll eat about any way you can get the food into them."

Running a hand through Maggie's tear-streaked bangs, Nina's smile slipped.

"How much trouble are you and this baby's mother in, honey?"

A sob escaped before Maggie could stop it, Nina's unconditional support churning up the emotions she'd sucked down so she could keep moving.

It felt like she'd been running for days, rather than only the last few hours. She had to stop. She had to think for a minute. *Face facts. Use your head, Maggie.* Milk in a plastic bag was a miracle, but it wasn't getting Max any closer to his grandparents.

"Nina." She blinked away the next rush of tears. "I need your help. But you have to promise—"

"Shh," Nina crooned, pulling Maggie and the eagerly suckling Max into her arms. "Let's see what we can do for this little one, then we'll figure everything out. Does your family know you're here?"

"YOU EXPECT ME TO BELIEVE you don't know where Maggie is?" Angie sat on the edge of the teen's bed and held up Max's sock. "Fifteen minutes ago, you were telling me she hadn't been home all morning."

They didn't have time for this. Regulations, and protocol and doing her job aside, every second Maggie was out in the open put the girl more at risk. Not to mention, it gave Sam more of a chance to get away, if Maggie knew something that could help them nail the guy.

"I admitted Maggie was here, all right!" Tony stopped pacing and faced her. He dialed the portable phone again. Scowled as it rang, then ended the call and refocused on her. "Maggie was here. And she was scared to death, and covered in blood and—"

"Blood! Why didn't you call it in?"

"I didn't have time!" He tossed the phone to the bed. "She got here like five minutes before you did, and it took me that long to calm her and the baby down and get some sense out of her."

"So, she does have Max with her."

"Yeah. She brought him here, hoping I would help. Instead, I managed to convince her she couldn't trust me." His shoulders slumped. "Now, she's not even answering her cell phone."

"Why on earth did she run in the first place? Why not wait for the police to arrive?" It was close to impossible to watch Tony come unglued like this. She steadied herself against the urge to comfort him. Facts first. Being a friend would have to wait. "Why did she take the baby from the apartment?"

Tony stared straight through her again.

"That's it." She stood and unhooked her comlink from her belt. "Maggie can tell me herself when we find her—"

"No!" Tony was beside her in an instant. "Please. She's running scared. I need time to find her and calm her down before you bring the department into this."

"Running from what?"

"Damn it, Angie, from what she saw! From what she heard! She took Max because she promised Claire she'd keep him safe. And she's ready to leave town with the kid if she has to. Give me a few hours to figure out where she is and talk her into coming in on her own. Don't set the hounds on her yet. There's no telling what she'd do in the state she's in. I think she's already tried to reach Claire's family."

He held up the slip of paper he'd jotted a number on.

"This is an out-of-town number Maggie dialed. When I tried it, it was disconnected. Maggie said she was going to contact Claire's parents, so they'd come get Max. So Sam and his family couldn't get their hands on the baby."

"What does she think the department would do, hand Max over to a drug dealer—"

"She's not thinking! Her friend was gunned down in front of her. She's terrified, and I don't think she realizes yet how much danger she's in. If she did, she wouldn't have left here alone."

Angie hung on each speck of information. Her hand snaked out to touch her friend's arm. A tiny tug, and he was sitting beside her. Having him close was like an addictive balm, after the sting of knowing he still didn't completely trust her.

"No one else knows she witnessed the shootings

yet, right?" The desperation in his question begged
Angie to say yes. Begged her to listen.

"I didn't radio in I was coming here." She
crumpled the slip of paper he'd given her, recalling
his earlier crack about her caring more about the
election than a scared teenager. "I was too worried
about Maggie to think straight."

"I know." He bumped his shoulder into hers, a
guy's apology. Then he took her hand. "I'm sorry,
Angie, really—"

"I know." She couldn't take his heart-in-his-eyes
apology and stay focused, so she made herself let his
hand go. A few more inches between them would be
a good idea, too. She couldn't make her body scoot
away, so she grabbed on to harsh realities to create
the distance she needed. "Running around town with
a baby she's not supposed to have might just get
Maggie killed, when someone realizes that means
she was at the apartment this morning."

"Then help me find her before anyone else does."
The desperation in Tony's expression drew her in
even further. "Help me protect my niece."

She gave up her fight not to put her arms around
him. Focusing on only the job had never seemed
more impossible. Tony's initial resistance melted into
the kind of rib-crushing hug that confirmed how
much he'd needed the comfort she was offering.

No man had ever felt more right in her arms.

She had seen him like this once before. Last year, when his sister-in-law had had her liver transplant. Angie had been there as Tony watched Eric and his new family leave for New York for the procedures. It was the first time she'd glimpsed the shadows lurking beneath Tony's easygoing shell. The first time he'd trusted her enough to talk about the fear of one more person he'd let himself love being taken away.

I still have nightmares about losing my dad, he'd said, though she'd never gotten him to talk much about them. Bad dreams full of anger and guilt and helplessness that no doubt seemed to be coming true all over again.

"Maggie's going to be okay," Angie assured him.

"Not if we don't find her." He eased away and pulled his bottom lip between his teeth. A bottom lip Angie was close enough to see tremble. "I...I can't do this without you, Angie."

So, now they were a *we.* She braced for the panic that had filled her two nights ago, but this time her second thoughts were convenient no-shows. And that's when she realized she'd decided to keep Tony's secrets the moment he'd opened that front door and she'd guessed how much trouble he was in.

Ladies and gentlemen, I give you Angie Carter. Hard-ass, all-business candidate for small-town sheriff.

"Okay. What do you need me to do?" she asked through the chaos her world had become.

Tony's warmth beside her was an unwanted reminder of how cold life was when he wasn't around. She'd made her career her only focus for years. Now, finding Tony's niece, making sure his family was okay, so he'd be okay, seemed far more important.

He was more dangerous to her than a hundred armed drug dealers.

"Angie…" His breath fanned her cheek. "Thank you. I—"

"Don't." Her palm lingered on his shoulder. She made herself push away. Ashamed for feeling anything but urgency to find first Maggie and Max, and then Sam Walker, she refused to need Tony's arms around her again. "Don't thank me. Help me figure out where to start."

"We need to find Claire's parents." He nodded to the scrap of paper clenched in her fist. "Maggie said they were living in Virginia the last time Claire saw them."

"HAVE YOU SEEN MAGGIE?" Tony asked Oliver Wilmington.

When he found his niece, he was going to hug her senseless. Then he was going to give serious thought to locking her in her room until her parents got back.

The Wilmington family butler, Robert, had

ushered Tony into the old man's enormous study, then he'd made himself scarce. Wilmington frowned at Tony from across a desk that took up half the room.

"Why would I have seen my great-granddaughter at this hour?" he asked, his mahogany chair squeaking as he resettled his weight. He checked the pocket watch attached by a gold chain to his vest— the man was dressed in a three-piece suit at nine o'clock on a Saturday morning. "Carrinne and Eric haven't been gone a full day, and you've already misplaced their daughter?"

After a lifetime of misunderstanding and distance, Maggie's mom and the grandfather who'd raised her were slowly rebuilding their relationship. They didn't keep each other on speed dial, but they were a family again. So the Wilmington mansion had been Tony's first stop. If he was lucky, Maggie was cooling her heels somewhere in this monstrous place, rethinking how pointless it had been to run in the first place.

Tony made himself chuckle and lean a nonchalant hip against the doorjamb.

"Maggie lit out of the house a little while ago." He checked his own watch, calculating how much time he dared let pass before calling his brother. "I need to find her, and I thought she might have come here. Doesn't she hang out in your solarium some weekends?"

"Reginald lets her help with the seedlings, yes. It's amazing, actually, how much she enjoys the plants. Just like her mother…" Wilmington's eyes lost a bit of their focus. Carrinne's return to Oakwood had changed them all, but maybe the grandfather, who'd once disowned her, most of all. The old man's attention returned to Tony. "Why don't you try reaching her on that infernal cell phone that's always growing out of the girl's ear. Kids these days never go anywhere without one of those things."

"That's Maggie." Tony forced an easy smile. "But she's not answering." He'd left at least five messages, calmly trying talk her in. Hoping each time that she'd answer, maybe trust him enough to call back. "Any ideas where I could get my hands on her?"

Wilmington's bushy eyebrows drew together. With a thud, he closed the ledger he'd been reviewing.

"What's happened?" he asked.

Tony blinked, not about to share a single detail of the morning's events.

Wilmington had never liked Eric or their dad. The man rarely bothered to notice when Tony was in the room. As if Tony cared, beyond whether the old geezer's behavior upset his sister-in-law. But Angie could only run interference with the department for an hour, maybe two. By noon, when she'd made it back to the station after visiting the crime scene, she expected him to have Maggie and the baby waiting in her office—

"Deputy Rivers! I have a right to know what's going on."

As the richest, most influential man in three counties, Wilmington thought he had a right to pretty much anything he wanted.

"We were supposed to work on a project for school." Tony flashed a smile full of *it's-no-big-deal*. He threw in another shrug to round things out. "It's due for a final grade on Monday, and I thought I'd have all weekend to help her. Now it looks like I'll be on duty this afternoon, and I can't reach Maggie on her cell. Have you seen her?"

Wilmington's stare stretched a few seconds beyond mild curiosity. He'd never been a warm man, particularly not to a Rivers. And he still didn't trust either Tony or his brother. Never would, was Tony's guess.

"There's an emergency at the department?" the old man asked.

"What?"

"You said they're calling you in on the weekend. Is there a problem? I've been buried here with quarterly taxes all morning. I haven't heard a thing from town."

"Not really." Tony let go of the smile. What did it matter what the old man thought? "We're a little shorthanded with Eric away. So have you seen Maggie or not?"

"Not since last weekend." The man's cool appraisal said he knew he wasn't getting the whole story. He seemed to be weighing his words carefully, though. Like it or not, they were family. Perhaps not the family Wilmington would have chosen for Carrinne, but family all the same.

Tony's family.

Stop trying to handle this alone.

He turned away. Sprinting to his truck held a certain appeal. One minute he was hugging Angie, practically coming apart in her arms. The next, his dysfunctional ties to Oliver Wilmington were starting to sound like grounds for taking the man into his confidence.

He turned to leave.

"Guess I'll ask if Robert's seen her," he said over his shoulder.

"Deputy?" Nina, the Wilmington cook and overseer of all things domestic in the mansion, motioned him down the hall and farther out of her employer's earshot.

As Tony neared the dining room, she led him beneath the cover of the arched stairway that led to the second floor.

"Nina, have you seen—"

The elderly woman raised a finger to her lips. The other hand, he noticed, held a paper grocery sack. The edges were rolled down to cover its contents.

She glanced behind him then stepped close enough to whisper, "You need to come with me."

"LOOKS LIKE SHE WAS PACKING to go somewhere," Deputy Buddy Tyler said, using the tip of a ballpoint pen to sift through the overstuffed bags on the bed.

"Hmm," Angie repeated for what she was sure was the hundredth time.

At best, her silence about Maggie's involvement was a breach of departmental protocol, even though the decision was well within her discretion as chief and acting sheriff. At worst, delaying sending her guys out to find the girl was giving Sam Walker time to tunnel further underground.

But she'd promised Tony a couple of hours. And so far, she'd seen nothing at the scene to cause her to change her mind. Nothing they couldn't get a handle on from the evidence at hand. Talking Maggie in gently, so her statement would do the most good, still seemed the best for everyone involved. At least that was the rationalization that kept Angie going.

She glanced to where Gary Simpson, the county medical examiner, was finishing his on-site investigation. He drew a sheet over Claire Morton's body as Angie approached.

"What have you got for me?" She couldn't take her eyes off the prone figure of the troubled girl she'd spoken to yesterday afternoon.

"Single gunshot to the chest. Clipped her aortic valve is my guess. She bled out within minutes." He motioned into the closet. "The shot definitely came through the wall from the other room. Can't tell yet if it's from the gun the other victim was holding. I examined him first, and the abrasions on his knuckles suggest physical blows were exchanged. His gun's been fired. But whoever he was fighting could have shot the bullet that killed this one."

She nodded. Buddy Tyler walked over.

"What do we have on the other shooter?" she asked him. "What's our status?"

"The dead man's ID says Marcus Long. It lists an Atlanta address."

"There's no unexplained blood that we can find," Martin Rhodes interjected before Buddy could say more. He joined the group from where he'd been searching through Claire's bedside table for clues on how to contact her family. "Except the residue that left someone's prints on the phone, my guess when the 911 call was placed. There's one slug in the wall out there, probably from the victim's gun. The trajectory of the bullet that took out the girl fits with it coming from somewhere else in the room."

"What about in here?" Angie asked them both.

"Lots of drug paraphernalia," Rhodes replied over his partner. "No narcotics. No other weapons. Am I the only one who thinks the baby not being here doesn't fit?"

Rhodes made a production of searching through the diaper tote sitting beside a bulging bag of baby clothes. The fact that he didn't bother to elaborate on his last statement meant Angie was going to have to pry the information out of him.

What a surprise.

Martin Rhodes deferred to her position as his superior only when given a direct order. Otherwise, she might as well not be in the room. After her promotion, his not-quite-friendly grudge toward her had taken a turn toward uncooperative, progressing lately into a full-fledged chip on his shoulder.

"What doesn't fit?" she asked, though she'd rather they focused on anything else.

"Why are all the baby's things here, if the kid's not?" He riffled through a bunny-covered diaper bag. "Mom's got everything but the crib packed, like she was taking the kid somewhere. Her wallet and cell phone are here… Wipes, diapers, formula. But no baby."

He pointed toward the stuffed duffel on the floor,

as if he were teaching a lesson in Remedial Investigation 101, and Angie were too green to appreciate the obvious. She'd love to publicly call the guy on being a condescending jerk, but covering for Tony and Maggie came first.

"Now I don't have a woman's intuition and all," Rhodes reasoned. "But I'd say maybe there was a baby here after the shooting, like the dispatcher thought. And someone left with it in a mighty big hurry. You follow me?"

"Maybe the father has him?" Buddy, a first-year straight out of the academy in Atlanta, glanced hesitantly between Angie and Rhodes. The tension seething between his morning ride partner and the chief wasn't lost on the kid.

"Or somebody else." Rhodes puffed out his burly chest, as if he'd solved a riddle only Sherlock Holmes could untangle. "Someone who witnessed what went down, then hightailed it to safer ground. The dispatcher said the caller sounded like an adolescent female. Maybe one of the parents' friends has the kid. That would give us an eyewitness. Unless, of course, you have another take on it, Chief."

"We got an APB out on Sam Walker?" she asked Buddy, refusing to be baited.

"Like that's going to get us anywhere." Rhodes shuffled away to search the apartment some more.

"We'll find him, Chief." Buddy frowned at his partner's sarcasm. "We'll bring the son of a bitch in."

Angie nodded as she gazed around the room. At the electronic scale her deputies had dug out of the front closet. It was sophisticated enough to precisely measure even the smallest items—like bags of crystal meth. Along with it had come a case of tiny baggies and containers. The kind used to hold and distribute street drugs.

Sam had been careful. They hadn't found a speck of anything illegal in the apartment. But there were discarded cell phones and beepers everywhere, each of them currently being printed and recorded by her men. Sam Walker's link, no doubt, to the runners, dealers and clients that kept a thriving drug circuit going.

And mixed in with the chilling reality of how dangerous the man was, were bits and pieces of Claire Morton's life. Pastel clothing littered every flat surface. Her things and her baby's. Stuffed animals and toys she'd used to entertain Max, cuddled up next to the tools of the drug trade. A desperate attempt to create a normal life amid a nightmare.

A nightmare Angie should have stopped before it had gotten a young girl killed.

Racket from the front room announced the arrival of the paramedics and the stretcher that would transport Claire and the other victim to the waiting ambulance, and then on their lonely ride to the morgue. Frustration and regret always accompanied that sound for Angie, now more than ever. Because there was still a girl out there in danger. And a town full of teenagers just like Maggie and Claire, who deserved to grow up untouched by all this crap.

"A reporter from the evening news is at the door," Buddy announced, returning from ushering the paramedics into the bedroom. "The mayor's talking with them. You want me to—"

"No press, damn it!" How could Henderson stomach making a political play at a time like this?

"Now there's a switch." Rhodes chuckled. "You passing on a prime opportunity for some no-frills campaigning."

"All I care about is finding our second shooter," she hissed. She'd forgiven Tony for questioning her loyalty. Rhodes was a different matter. "Which you aren't going to do loitering around here. Get back to the station and have your on-site reports on my desk pronto. If that's too much work for you, let me know. I'm sure I can find someone else to finish things up."

"What about the mayor?" Buddy crossed his arms and scowled at his partner. He jerked his head toward the sound of Henderson's booming voice playing to the cameras outside.

"I'll take care of the mayor." A pointed look made

sure she still had Rhodes's attention. "No comment of any kind from the department until we've got more to go on. Let Sam Walker think he's still one step ahead of us. Make sure the rest of the guys understand that. I want the details to stay in-house, until we've apprehended our man."

Until I have Maggie Rivers safe and sound, down at headquarters giving her statement.

"It's your call, boss," Buddy nodded his support.

"Once you've wrapped up the paperwork, start with Walker's family. Not that I think they're likely to tell us where he is."

"Any other bright ideas on how to find our perp after we exhaust the obvious?" Rhodes quipped.

"Surprise me with your creativity." Her tone announced where the jackass could shove his attitude. She knelt beside the girl she'd played Nintendo with almost every Friday afternoon at the youth center. "Just have Sam Walker in a cell at the station by the end of the day."

"Yes, sir." Rhodes's surly *sir* on his way out of the room could just as easily have been another word. One of the four-letter variety.

Angie pulled back the sheet and stared at Claire's still form, shutting out everything else. Helping get Claire's baby away from Sam Walker and his family had never seemed more right. Maggie was hiding an infant from Family Services, where Max should be at that very minute, but Angie didn't care. The hell with the ramifications, the regs or the chance that her decision might cost her the election once the mayor found out.

Making sheriff didn't even rate a second thought. If getting the top spot meant dragging Maggie Rivers in, or not doing right by Claire's baby, then Angie didn't want it. Her job was to protect the citizens of Oakwood, simple as that.

Tony had reached the same conclusion sooner. His recklessness had frustrated the hell out of her an hour ago, even as his fear for Maggie had won her over. Now, she was damn glad to have the man in her corner.

But if Maggie or the baby got hurt, or if the department somehow lost Sam Walker because Angie waited too long to take the girl's statement, Angie would never forgive herself. The violent strong-hold drugs had on Oakwood had to end, and it had to end now.

People she cared about were in danger, and she had to protect them, whether it meant doing things by the book or not. She smoothed a hand across Claire's still-soft cheek, grieving for the girl's mother, wherever the woman was.

Had it really been only yesterday when her biggest worry had been whether or not to make a habit of kissing Tony Rivers?

CHAPTER SEVEN

MAGGIE HAD TO THINK.

Why couldn't she think!

She'd always believed she was strong, like her mom, and dad and uncle. Now look at her. Strong people didn't fall apart like this. All she had to show for hours of protecting Max was no food for the baby, no diapers and no clue what to do next.

Stupid!

She redialed the number on her cell phone. The one she'd tried first at her house. As if it would actually work this time. Wherever Claire's parents were, they no longer lived where Virginia information thought they did.

So why keep dialing it, you dodo?

Her fingers danced a new pattern on the tiny number pad. Her mom's cell-phone number filled the display. Her thumb hovered over Send, then a flick cleared the screen. Calling her parents meant giving up Max, and she couldn't do that.

Nina would be back soon with some things for the baby. And she'd no doubt be ready for round two of why Maggie shouldn't be doing what she was doing. But the housekeeper hadn't blinked an eye before shooing her and Max to Great-Grandfather Wilmington's dilapidated overseer's cottage.

Secluded at the back edge of the wooded, ten-acre estate that took up an entire downtown block of Governor's Square, the tiny house looked like a shack from the outside. But its rooms had been kept up. Clean and quiet, with running water and electricity, but no TV or telephone, it was the perfect hideaway. Best of all, it was invisible to anyone who might walk by on the street. Nina had said most people in town didn't even know it was there. Maggie hadn't had a clue.

Not having a clue was big for her right now.

She'd ditched her uncle without giving him a chance to ditch Angie first. Now she'd never know if he'd meant to hide her like she'd asked. *Stupid.* Angie herself could have helped, if Maggie had only talked with the woman last night, instead of keeping Claire's secrets. *Stupid.* And she'd crept over here, keeping to side streets and hoping not to be seen, all for what? So she could keep dialing the same dead number over and over again?

She redialed the Mortons' digits from memory.

The same recording as before mocked her. Ending the call with a muted scream, she peeked over her shoulder at the sleeping baby curled, diapered-butt in the air, atop a blanket on the faded couch.

Max was finally peaceful, while Claire was out there somewhere fighting for her life. The sounds and horrible scene from that morning came crashing back. Maggie squeezed her hands into fists. Fought off the panicky, hiccuping kind of crying she knew she couldn't let happen, or she'd never stop.

Claire had been hurt bad. She was… Maybe she was even…

God! She couldn't think that.

Claire would be fine, and needed Maggie to do what she'd promised. Max needed her. She was a smart kid, raised in one of the toughest cities in the country. She could handle this. She could get Max to his grandparents. And as helpful as Nina was being, the older woman had seemed on the verge of turning her in.

Which meant Maggie couldn't stay here long.

Come on. Think. Stop running scared and use your brain.

Tony had been on her side, or at least leaning in that direction. He'd probably checked on Claire by now. Would he help if she asked him again?

Did she really have a choice?

She glanced at her phone's display. He'd left six

messages already. Calling him back would be the scariest conversation of her life, with the last person on earth she'd ever thought she'd be afraid of.

She sat on the cushion beside Max and rubbed his back through the baby-soft shirt her friend had dressed him in that morning. Touching a living, breathing tie to Claire, she smiled sadly. Max's face, relaxed in sleep, was so precious. And her friend had given him to Maggie to protect.

She dialed her uncle's number. If this was a mistake, what was one more disaster piled on top of the rest of the day? Doing this alone when she didn't have to was stupid.

"U...Uncle Tony?" she said as soon as the call connected, her voice so broken up she wouldn't have recognized it. "It's Maggie. I'm at my great-grand-father's. Could... Could you come and get—"

The front door swooshed open before she could finish.

Startled, she jumped to her feet, dropping the cell phone. Then before she realized what she was doing, she was flying across the room and into her uncle's arms.

"...DRUG PARAPHERNALIA ALL OVER the apartment!" Uncle Tony shouted twenty minutes later. He was as close to losing it as Maggie had ever seen him.

Tony never raised his voice like this. Never paced like her dad did, when he was worrying through something important. Tony was always so together. So, *whatever, no big deal*.

"You tripped over a dead body," he ranted on. "After you almost got shot right along with your friend. And you had no idea Sam Walker was dealing crystal meth? How could you not know, Maggie? These are dangerous people."

"I thought Sam was a jerk, but I didn't know he was into drugs. Not before last night!" she snapped from where she'd squared off across the room, holding Max against her like a shield.

She'd cried when Tony had first gotten there. Her tears and self-pity were thankfully gone now. She was pissed instead, and pissed felt a whole lot better.

"I get it, okay," she said. "I messed up!"

A snuffling sound floated up from the baby in her arms. Maggie held her breath. Jiggled Max. Prayed for a miracle. But, no dice.

A full-fledged wail made both her and her uncle wince.

"Now look what you did." She laid the bottle she'd been feeding Max on the coffee table and cuddled him onto her shoulder.

Nina had produced the formula from the bag of stuff she'd lifted from her niece's nearby home. And

Max had been happily siphoning the contents of the bottle ever since Maggie had nubbed it against his lips—the way she'd seen Claire do. Patting the baby's back, soothing his upset, Maggie's anger-induced high faded. Images of Claire doing the same motherly task took over.

Nina's worried gaze melted into a concerned smile as Maggie blinked away fresh tears. A very un-baby-like belch saved her from completely losing it. Followed by the sickening sensation of warm, slimy ooze trailing down her neck, then between her shoulder blades.

"Ew," she complained at the same time that Max gave a relieved giggle. She returned him to the crook of her arm, where he began to kick for more formula. "You knew I didn't have anything to change into, didn't you?"

Her lame attempt at scolding earned another giggle as she once again plugged the baby's mouth with the bottle. With her free hand, she patted at the goo decorating her upper back.

"Ew," she repeated, still ignoring her uncle, who she hadn't been able to make herself stop hugging a few minutes ago.

Nina stepped away from the corner she'd been lurking in since walking Tony over from the main house. The woman hadn't bothered apologizing for outing Maggie. But she had hung around, an unofficial buffer between Maggie and her increasingly irate uncle.

"Let me finish feeding the baby and put him in a fresh diaper." Nina produced a box of baby wipes from the paper sack and handed several to Maggie. "You two need your privacy, and I have to head back to the mansion before too long. Sooner or later, your great-grandfather's going to notice I'm MIA."

And just like that, Maggie's buffer was heading into one of the two tiny bedrooms off the den, taking Max with her.

"What do you mean, you knew Sam was into drugs last night?" A scary calm had filled Tony's voice.

Maggie almost wished he was still yelling.

When he'd held her when he'd first come in, he'd been shaking almost as badly as she had. *Thank God,* he'd repeated over and over again. *Thank God, you're all right. Thank God…*

But that was before he'd insisted they call her parents. Before she'd refused. Actually, she'd threatened to run with Max again, which had prompted an *over my dead body* response that had been so not her uncle, she hadn't been able to hold back a snort. Which had pretty much ended the warm and fuzzy stuff.

Then the inquisition had begun.

"Maggie?"

"What?" She stalled by dabbing at her shoulder with the baby wipes.

She was in trouble. A lot of trouble. Her uncle was her best shot at getting Max out of Oakwood. Except he wanted her to give up. And giving up sounded so tempting....

"Did you know how dangerous Sam and this guy he killed were? Did you know about the drugs?"

When her silent glance confirmed it, her uncle bit his bottom lip and gave his shoes a five-second stare before he looked back up.

"Why didn't you say something to your dad?" he demanded. "And why the hell did you run from me? Angie came this morning because she's worried sick about you. She wants to help. Do you have any idea what Sam's people will do to you, if they find out you're a witness to two homicides?"

"I—" Her uncle's words slammed into her. "Two what? You... You mean Claire— No! she was alive when I left. The ambulance was on its way...."

Oh God!

She couldn't breathe.

Two homicides.

Do you have any idea what Sam's people will do to you...

With a silent scream of denial, she curled inward, the pain crushing her.

"Damn, honey. I'm so sorry." Her uncle's voice and arms surrounded her. He eased her onto the couch cushions that were still warm from Max's nap. Then he pulled her into a frightening hug. The kind of hug that said he wished he could lie to her, but he couldn't. "Claire was already gone when the EMTs arrived at the apartment. I'm so sorry. I know it hurts, and you're scared. But you're safe now. You and Max both. Angie's covering for us until we can get you to a secure location. No one knows you were at the apartment yet, or that you have the baby, or even that I came here."

Tony tipped his niece's chin up and waited until she made eye contact. He had to find a way to get through to her.

"I'm sorry about your friend, but we don't have much time," he said. "Angie can't keep your part in what happened quiet for long, not without inter- fering with the investigation. And I can't ask her to do that. But once you make a statement down at the station—"

"No!" Tears choked Maggie's words. "No… No station. I have to get Max out of here. I promised Claire…. I—"

A trembling hand covered her mouth.

"Oh my God. She's gone. Claire's really gone!"

"Shh," Tony soothed, rocking her gently, cursing

himself for knowing a hell of a lot more about high fives than hugs. "I know it's a shock. I know how close you and Claire were. Let it out, honey. We're going to make this okay. For you and for Max. I don't know how, Mags, but we're going to make this okay."

She nodded against his shoulder. He took it as a good sign when her breathing began to calm. Maggie was nothing short of a hero for what she'd sacrificed for her mom. The painful surgery and recovery she'd endured voluntarily. Tony's money was on the hero inside his niece finding a way through her grief now, so they could make the right choices for her friend's baby.

Swallowing as if she were about to vomit, still sniffling, she pushed away and stumbled to her feet. She squeezed her hands into fists, and for a second it looked as if her shaking knees were going to dump her back down to the couch.

When she finally squared her shoulders, Tony wanted to applaud.

"I'll tell you what I know," she said. "And I'll make a full statement to whoever you want later. Whatever you need to put Sam and his goons behind bars. I heard plenty at the apartment, and Claire told me more. But I'll talk on only one condition."

"What condition?" Everything inside Tony turned cold at the reckless determination in her voice. "Maggie, I've been patient. I haven't called your folks yet, because I want you to know you can trust me. But I swear to God, keep playing these games, and you'll be talking with my brother in about sixty seconds!"

She grabbed the cell phone he'd pulled from his jeans.

"One condition," she repeated, flashing her mother's New York City frown. "You help me get Max to Claire's parents before I come in. Before anyone else knows I have him. Help me get Max away from Oakwood, and I'll do anything you want."

"Away?" He stood, looming over her. "Maggie, Max's life is in danger every second he stays with you, don't you get that? Because *you're* in danger. When Sam Walker comes looking for you—and he will, as soon as he suspects you're the one who ran from the apartment with his kid—he's not going to let a little thing like his baby being in the way stop him. The department has evidence he's dealing now. He's a murder suspect, and you're the ace up our sleeve for nailing the bastard. Once he knows that, you're his next target. The safest place for both you and Max is down at the station, where we can keep an eye on you. It's not like we're going to give the baby back to Sam. Let Angie track his grandparents down. Family Services will take good care of Max until—"

"No! They won't be able to keep him away from Sam's family."

"You don't know that. I can talk with the social worker—"

"You can guarantee me that only Claire's parents will be able to take him?"

"No." *Lie to her, man. Just lie to her and bring her in. Worry about making it up to her later.* Only he couldn't. Halfway caring and easy fixes had already done enough damage to his relationship with his niece. Maggie got the truth from now on, no matter what. "But—"

"No. No buts. I won't do it. I promised Claire to get her baby out of Oakwood."

"You won't— I'm not giving you a choice, honey. You're a witness to a homicide, and you've fled a crime scene. Technically, you're already guilty of kidnapping. And Angie's ass is on the line every second she covers for you. Max doesn't belong to you. You have to give him up!"

"I'm…" Maggie wiped her eyes. "I'm not going to let Claire down again. Can't you understand that? I'm not going to fail Max, the way I failed his mother, because I'm scared and it's easier to quit."

Tony cupped her wet cheek in his palm, bursting inside with pride, despite everything. "You didn't fail Claire. None of this is your fault. And I know you're not a quitter. God, you and your mom are the strongest fighters I've ever met. I'm so proud of you, and how you're willing to sacrifice for the people you love. But a fighter always looks for the smart way through. And more than anything, you're smart. You got Max out of that apartment, in case Sam came back. You've kept him safe all this time. You found Nina. You called me, once you had a minute to think. You're amazing, Maggie."

"Then you understand." She threw her arms around him. "I have to keep doing what I can for Max."

He set her away, his head shaking. "So what's your next move, since you're so determined to do this on your own? I got the grandparents' number from your bedroom phone. I know it's been disconnected. What's next, traipsing cross-country with a baby that's not yours, looking for people you've never met who don't even know you're coming?"

She had no plan, he could tell. But the terrifying thing was he could also see her determination to keep trying. He held out his hand for his cell phone and prayed.

"Let me call Angie, and she'll meet us back at her office. From there, we'll figure out what to do to protect both you and Max."

"No. Angie doesn't have a say here."

"Maybe not." He gave up waiting and grabbed the phone back. "But I do. Sam Walker is a fugitive, and he's running scared. Sooner or later he'll figure out you're a liability. You're not going anywhere but to the station."

"Try and stop me." She headed for the bedroom door Nina had closed to give them some privacy. But she didn't make it two feet before he'd planted himself directly in her path.

"I love you, Maggie." The room vibrated the words he'd never said to her before. *And exactly why haven't you ever said it, you dumb ass?* "And I understand how upset you are about your friend. I lost people I loved when I was younger than you are, and… And I know how that can feel." His eyes misted as every messed-up piece of his life flashed before them. "I get how awful everything is right now. How responsible you feel for Claire. How alone you feel… You're my family." His voice deepened with the strain of saying things he'd always thought better left unsaid. "I feel responsible for you, the same as you do for Max. I won't let you put yourself at risk, no matter how good you think your reasons are. I'd die before I let anything happen to you. Understand? There's no way in hell I'm letting you run from me again."

"I…I love you, too, Tony." She took a hesitant step

closer, then fell into his arms, hugging him with shocking strength. "And I don't want to run. But there's no way in hell I'm risking Max going anywhere near Sam, or his family."

Tony swallowed his niece's declaration of love. Maggie's commitment to put herself at risk for her friend's child was as rock solid as his inability to let her do it alone.

"You said fighters always look for a way through." She stepped away. "Well, that's what I'm trying to do. Please, Uncle Tony. I know I've screwed this up so far, but we can fix it together. I know we can. Don't make me bring Max in until we reach Claire's parents. What difference would a few more hours make?"

CHAPTER EIGHT

"YOU READY TO GO?" Angie's sister asked as she breezed through the door to Angie's office twenty minutes after Tony Rivers's promised check-in time.

What Angie was ready for was to wring one tall, dark and tardy deputy's neck. Or maybe she'd call Tony's brother and let Eric deal with this. She was already pushing it, not calling her boss before now—"

"Ange?" Lissa frowned. "We're still on for lunch, aren't we?"

The normalcy of the burgers and chocolate shakes they always ordered sounded like the perfect escape. Hanging with Lissa was her only guilt-free family time these days.

"Sorry," she winced. "I'm buried in a tough case right now, and I—"

"You have to take care of it before you can get away," Lissa said at the same time as Angie. "Now where have I heard that before?"

"Melissa, please." Angie picked up the phone to check her voice mail. Maybe she'd missed Tony's call.

"Oh, I remember now." Her sister pressed the button to drop the line. "That's exactly what you said last Wednesday, when you weaseled out on having dinner with the family."

"Lissa—"

"A very important dinner, if you'll recall."

"Cut it out." Angie redialed voice mail, her glare daring her perpetually adorable sister even to think about touching the phone again.

One year older, Melissa was the closest to Angie's status as the youngest of the Carter girls. They'd grown up practically twins—had even gone through school in the same grade, since they were born in October and then the following June, when Angie had insisted on arriving a month early. But a casual observer would have a hard time picturing the two of them coming from the same womb.

What with the blond curls Lissa had gotten from their mother, and the ultrafeminine clothes she wore, compared to Angie's straight brown mane, pulled back into a work ponytail, and her uniform shirt and slacks that had been designed, it seemed, to hide every last hint of a woman's curves. In their family's eyes, Melissa was as close to perfect as a daughter got. The gorgeous earth mother of two equally beautiful girls who were the apple of their grand-parents' eyes.

Angie on the other hand...

"I'm sorry I missed dinner." Her explanation lacked grace and even a hint of true regret. "But I had—"

"Work that needed to get done?" Lissa's sweet smile made the judgment sting even more. "*Important* work, no doubt. Much more important, say, than your niece's second birthday party?"

Angie set the phone back onto its receiver as a recorded voice informed her there were no messages in her in-box.

Little Callie's party.

"Oh, Lissa." She closed her eyes.

Skipping Wednesday's dinner had meant another week away from her family's ongoing disappoint-ment with her life choices since her engagement had fallen apart. Another discussion about how her job and bid for sheriff were taking over her life. She'd spent the night knocking out a report for Eric instead, cross-coding details from each drug arrest they'd made. Important information, but she'd also forgot-ten her niece's birthday.

"I'm so sorry. It's been crazy around here, trying to get a handle on this drug situation, or I never would have forgotten."

"It's always crazy around here, Angie. And when

you don't show up where you're supposed to be, it's always about your job." Lissa was usually the most understanding, the most accepting of the whole Carter brood. "I know you're a champ at bringing order to chaos. It's the outside world you're not so good at handling anymore."

"Don't start." Angie squirmed in her chair.

"If you do make sheriff, what about your personal life? You're already working around the clock. You've shut yourself off from everything else. You never have fun anymore."

Hearing their parents' words spewing out of her sister's mouth was the one thing that could have made Angie's day worse.

"How I live my life is my decision," she argued. "And my job—"

"Your job *is* your life, Ange." Lissa placed her oversize mom-bag on the edge of the desk, then sat herself in the squeaky guest chair. Perched with her back straight and her delicate features composed in ladylike affront, she managed to make the ugly wooden thing look like a throne. "And I understand why. I've always understood. Ever since Freddie dumped you, you're determined to make anything except your personal life your priority—"

"I'm not talking about Freddie today."

Or any other day.

She'd tried building a happy family of her own, with her dream *family* man. Then out-of-control endometriosis had led to an emergency hysterectomy six months before her wedding, and had put an end to the children part of the dream. Her fiancé had never rallied. Turned out, he'd loved the idea of a big family, like the one she'd grown up in, more than he'd actually loved her.

And he hadn't simply dumped her. He'd waited until everything but the rehearsal dinner was over. She'd had shower gifts and wedding presents to return. A nonrefundable wedding dress to hide in a closet while she paid it off over the next year. Way too many family and friends to explain why the wedding hadn't happened. Why she hadn't been woman enough for the man who'd promised her the rest of his life.

Humiliation and heartache hounding her, she'd turned to the place in her world where she'd always been enough, nonfunctioning ovaries be damned. She'd spent the last three years hyperfocused on what she did best, culminating in a promotion to chief and the pending election.

Wishing Lissa were anywhere but sitting in her office, Angie pulled out the drawer that tucked her keyboard beneath the desk, opened her e-mail and checked for an update from her records search for

Claire's parents. She only scanned the messages flashing in her in-box, ignoring Mayor Henderson's continued fury at being escorted from Sam Walker's apartment that morning, complete with a demand for an update on the department's investigation.

She ground her teeth at the computer-generated time displayed on the monitor.

Where was Tony?

"All right, let's forget Freddie," her sister acquiesced. "Let's talk about how you're using your job to shut out everyone else in your life. Like your family. And what about friends? When was the last time you went out for a drink or dinner with a friend?"

Two nights ago, when I was crawling all over Tony Rivers!

A man she couldn't have and keep her dream of being elected sheriff, or even her job as chief for that matter. For years she hadn't been tempted to care about anything but work. Then her best friend had turned into the worst kind of distraction.

Memories from the Eight Ball heated all the places inside only Tony seemed able to touch. She slapped the keyboard tray back under her desk and pinned her sister with a glare.

"My job isn't replacing anything. And yes, it's my number-one focus right now. It has to be if I'm going have a shot at making sheriff."

Which was exactly the right sentiment to stop her skin from heating with memories, and start it crawling instead. Thanks to the mayor's escalating antics and her decision to bend the rules for Maggie and Tony, she'd never felt less passionate about winning the election.

Which left her where, exactly?

"How can you make work more important than family?" Lissa asked.

Her sister didn't look angry anymore. Her expression was too sad to be angry.

"I don't," Angie lied. She couldn't take this. Not today. Not from Lissa. "I missed dinner. I'm sorry. But it was just dinner."

"Is making sheriff really going to make you happy?" her sister pressed. "When all you have is an empty house waiting for you when you go home at night?"

"And exactly what are you suggesting I do? Quit and find myself a man to make me happy?" The memory of Freddie's bone-deep sadness as he'd broken off their engagement, then his beaming smile when she'd seen him out with Julie Sanders the very next week, came from out of nowhere. "I tried that already, remember? And when Freddie couldn't handle me being broken, the perfect life Mom and Dad promised would make us girls happy went up in flames. So save the lecture, Lissa. My life is bonfire free now, and I like it that way. I'm fine, so don't you dare feel sorry for me."

"Fine? Is *fine* really all you want? What if something happens, and you don't make sheriff. What then?"

"Then I'll work something else out." Panic bubbled up at the thought, rolling over the confidence Angie worked so hard to fake. "If I need to, I'll start over again. It's not like I haven't done it before!"

She shouted the last sentence, as much to her surprise as her sister's.

"Angie—" Lissa scooted closer to the edge of her chair. "I didn't—"

"I'm sorry I missed Callie's party." Angie wrestled her disastrous past, her crumbling present and her heart rate back into submission. "I promise, I'll make it up to her. And we'll reschedule lunch, once I—"

"I really didn't come here to upset you." Lissa's smile was sad, but beautiful as always. "I'm worried about you."

"Well don't. I like my life." At least she had, until a few months ago, when a certain deputy who needed to get his butt into her office had ambled his lean hips under her radar and tempted her to want more.

"You like your *job.*" Lissa pulled her purse from the desk and stood. "And you're working yourself to death, hoping that your election will be enough to make you forget about everything you're giving up."

"There's nothing wrong with working hard." Nothing wrong with wanting to forget.

"Sure there is, if it means hiding from the people in your life. People who love you too much, so you shut them out until they stop coming around."

Angie couldn't find the right words, whatever they were.

"I have a lot to do." She yanked her keyboard out again and trained her eyes on the computer screen. Willed them to focus as she began typing. "I'll call tomorrow. Maybe take Callie bowling or something later in the week."

"Ange…"

"We've got a major break brewing in this case," she said over the clatter of her fingers slapping computer keys. "Let's do burgers next Saturday."

The sister she hadn't fought with since age eight, when they'd stolen each other's Barbies, stood in front of her as silent as stone.

"I love you," Lissa finally said.

It had been years since Angie had been able to return the sentiment to anyone, even her favorite sister. Today was no different. She kept typing as her sister left, though her blurring vision made it impossible to read a single word.

Crying.

At work.

She really was losing it.

But it wasn't only her sister's guilt trip getting the best of her. It was Claire Morton and her baby, and Maggie and, God help her, it was her mixed up feelings for Tony Rivers.

Just how many ways did life plan to blow her calm, orderly world?

Her phone chose that moment to ring. Angie rubbed her eyes until she could read the caller ID.

It was about damn time!

Raising the receiver to her ear, she cleared her throat and thumbed the call through.

"Where the hell are you?" she groused.

"I found Maggie." Tony didn't sound nearly as relieved by the development as he should have.

Not a good sign.

"Then bring her in." Angie grabbed a hastily scribbled note from her desk. "I'm starting to get information about Claire's parents. It looks promising. But I can't put off calling Eric much longer. I know he'll want to talk with Maggie before she makes her statement."

"Don't call Eric yet."

An even worse sign.

"I've waited too long already." She checked her watch. Three hours since the 911 call from Walker's place. "I owe him a heads-up on the homicides. He almost canceled the trip yesterday, after that Reynolds kid OD'd. He'll want to be a part of bringing Sam in."

"Just hold off on calling him, all right?" Tony's sigh had *he couldn't believe he was doing this* written all over it. "I'll square things with my brother. I've found Maggie, but…"

"But…?" Why did she even bother to ask, when she already knew what he was about to say?

"But I can't bring her in. Not yet."

TONY GRIMACED at Angie's curse.

He was dragging her into even more trouble. But if she'd only hold off the department's investigation for a little while longer…

"I need more time," he mumbled into the phone as he let himself into his house.

Mumbled?

Twenty minutes of throwing in with his niece and this crazy scheme of hers, and Maggie had him mumbling.

"There is no more time," Angie said.

"Come on, Ange, work with me here. One more hour." He sprinted up the stairs to grab a fresh change of clothes for his niece. She'd stayed behind, covered in baby puke, safely hidden with Max at her great-grandfather's. "Maggie told me everything she heard at the apartment. Everything she knows about Sam and where he might be. I can give you the details, but she won't come in to make a formal statement until we track down Claire's parents. They need to be ready to work with Family Services from the start. I promised her.... I promised we'd find them before she had to bring Max in."

Perfectly logical, except there'd been nothing logical about his reaction to Maggie's pleas back at Wilmington's. He knew a little something about feeling helpless and powerless. How could he watch Maggie crumbling at the thought of failing her friend, hear her say she loved him and beg for his help, and stay logical?

"You promised her what?" Angie sputtered. "That baby belongs in county custody. And Maggie is a key witness to an ongoing murder investigation."

"I know." Tony pulled open a bureau drawer and began rummaging through shorts and his niece's favorite tank tops. "But—"

"No way," Angie kept her angry voice low. In an office made of paper-thin walls, you either spoke softly or shared your private conversation with the entire department. "No *buts*. Now. You're supposed to have Maggie in here now. Martin Rhodes is already working on the angle that someone was there during the shooting, and then left with the baby. I'm keeping the details out of the press, to keep Walker and his goons guessing about what we know. But anyone in the department who looks very hard is going to agree with Rhodes. Sam wouldn't have carted his baby with him when he ran from a homicide, which means someone else did. And that someone would logically be a friend of the mother's."

"All the more reason to keep Maggie safely out of it—"

"Not when she's a material witness. This department has a responsibility to the community to get the drugs off the street. In addition to protecting her, bringing Maggie in for questioning may get us one step closer to shutting Sam down."

"I told you, she's given me her statement—"

"And that's not good enough. You're personally involved in the case. The D.A.'s going to want to hear it from Maggie. Not to mention how the mayor's going to insist we both be fired, when he finds out we're obstructing an investigation."

"One more hour." He was asking her to put her job on the line. Her election. *You might just like a bit of carelessness in your life.* His own words, coming back to haunt him. "One more hour, and I'll have Maggie there. I'll find some way to get through to her. You said you had a lead on the Mortons?"

"Tony…" Angie sighed. He could picture the exasperated expression on her face. That sweet face he wanted to be close enough to touch again. "I'm as worried as you are about Maggie and Max's safety. If you'd only been there and seen Claire. Seen that apartment—"

Her voice broke on the last few words. Tony stopped digging for clothes and sat on the edge of Maggie's bed. How could someone who came off so tough be so soft and warm inside?

"I'm sorry, Angie. I'm so sorry about all of this."

Everything about the woman's bravery, her despair over a young girl's death, and her worry for Maggie and their community tempted him to cross a line that was unforgivable. Both because Angie was his boss, and because he'd only hurt her when he did what he always did in the end and walked away.

He didn't know how to make relationships last. He'd made it a point not to learn. And when Angie was finally ready to look for love again, she deserved better than another jackass good ol' boy as her consolation prize.

"The parents may have moved to Dallas," she finally said, her fight for composure tightening her voice. "I've tracked credit information, and I'll leave a couple of messages at the residence on file. Until they return my call, we won't know for sure, but I think we're onto something. Is that enough to convince Maggie that Max will be okay?"

"I... Maybe." Just maybe. "Let me ask her when I get back. It shouldn't be more than half an hour or—"

"Get back where? Why isn't Maggie with you? Where are you?"

"She's safe. I'm at my house, picking up a few things she needs. Then I—"

A sound that shouldn't be there cut him off. The warped step at the bottom of the stairs made that telltale squawk only when someone heavy walked on it.

"Tony?" Angie asked as he dropped the phone onto the bed, along with the clothes he'd picked out for Maggie.

He eased to the wall behind the bedroom door and withdrew his Beretta from where he'd tucked it inside the waistband of his jeans. He'd pulled his department-issued automatic from his glove compartment after leaving Wilmington's. For safety's sake, he'd told himself. No reason not to be extra cautious.

The next creak from the rickety stair agreed with him.

"Tony?" Angie's faint voice called from the discarded phone.

Then came a rustle. The almost imperceptible shift of movement at the top of the stairs.

Damn it. Who—

A leather-clad arm extended through the open

doorway, complete with a carbon copy of Tony's gun. Then whoever it was stalled, carefully taking in the room before stepping inside.

"I heard you up here, little girl," a man's voice said. "Don't bother to hide. There's nowhere to run this time."

Tony tensed. Soundlessly watched and waited. Laid the toe of his boot against the bottom of the door. Took a deep breath against the fury of knowing someone was in his home, in his niece's bedroom, with a gun drawn.

Diving into motion, he grabbed the extended arm with his free hand, using his foot to shove the door into the intruder at the same time. He yanked the man into the room and trained his weapon at the stranger's head for a kill shot.

"Freeze! Sheriff's department," he said out of habit, a split second before a blast fired from the hallway and all hell broke loose.

CHAPTER NINE

"WHAT KIND OF SHOW are you people running here?"
The mayor's voice boomed over the chaos swarming
the Rivers family's front yard.

Cruisers and assorted emergency vehicles had
screeched to rocking halts at odd angles up and down
the driveway and street. Curious neighbors stood
gawking beyond the yellow crime-scene tape that
corded off the perimeter. The local paper and evening
news reporters had beaten Angie there, alerted to the
excitement by police radio traffic.

And in the midst of it all, Angie refused to flinch
before the indignation of the most powerful man in
town. The last of her hopes for winning the sheriff's
spot were dying before her eyes, but all she could
think about was Tony. She needed to see for herself
that he wasn't hurt beyond the flesh wound the
county paramedics had reported.

"Mayor Henderson," she said, pulling herself
together enough to placate the man she'd already

pissed off once today. "If you'll give me a moment to explain—"

"Oh, I think I'm seeing things pretty clearly. By my count, you've racked up three dead bodies in as many days, one of them the teenage son of good friends of my wife. Then a runaway who was the live-in of a man you now tell me is probably at the heart of the drugs you people don't seem to be able to stomp out of my town. The second victim at that scene was a nice bonus. And now, we have what appears to be a B and E suspect on his way to Emergency with a bullet in his chest, put there courtesy of one of your off-duty deputies who has no explanation for what a pair of thugs were doing in his home in the first place. Sweetheart, it may be me, but I'm wondering if a few of these incidents are related."

"Yes, sir." Angie ignored the man's *sweetheart*. Oakwood was a small southern town. She switched back and forth between *Chief* and *sweetheart* often enough to develop a multiple personality disorder. "Of course there's a good chance the incidents are connected. But until now, we've had no solid leads that would allow us to nail our suspect. Now we have a deputy as an eyewitness saying that Sam Walker fired the shot that struck him, and we have another suspect on the way to the hospital. We're making excellent progress," she finished loud enough to be heard by the reporters her men had corralled behind the crime-scene ropes. She shot Cal Grossman a tight smile.

"So you've got it all wrapped up, do you?" Henderson was warming up to her verbal ass-whupping, either unaware or uncaring that most of her deputies were within hearing distance. From the smirk on Martin Rhodes's face, he was enjoying the show. "Except drugs are still pouring into our town. And gangs are shooting up the place every time I turn around. And, oh, there's the matter of Deputy Rivers's involvement in all of this, which I've yet to hear an explanation for."

"We're pretty sure this incident is connected to this morning's shootings." Make that *certain,* but that wasn't a conversation she planned to have in the open.

"How sure? Rivers wasn't even on duty today. Why would you think the shooting at his house is connected to the one from this morning?"

Angie scanned the crowd again, catching the attention of, among others, Buddy Tyler, Rhodes and the mayor's own son. Garret Henderson, trailing in his father's wake as usual, leaned in teenage insolence against a nearby pine tree. When he caught her watching, he spat at the ground beside his feet.

"Sir," she said to the boy's father. "We should table this discussion until we get to the precinct. I think—"

"No, we'll talk about it here."

Angie was bracing to argue further, when Tony stepped through the front door of the house. Wearing the same jeans and T-shirt as that morning, he was the most amazing thing she'd ever set eyes on. Sporting a makeshift bandage on his upper left arm, he was also less-than-tactfully refusing a paramedic's offer to step into a waiting ambulance.

His worried gaze tracked its way to her. Wordless understanding and relief passed between them, mixed with too much more for such a public stage.

Thank heavens, he was okay. And thank heavens Maggie hadn't returned to the house with him. Because Angie was confident that the men who'd shot at Tony had come for Maggie. Sam Walker had somehow made the connection between Tony's niece and that morning's shootings, and he'd made it far too quickly for there to be any other explanation than—

"Officer Carter!" Mayor Henderson demanded. At least he wasn't calling her *Chief* anymore, as if he'd just invented the title. "I'd like an answer to my question. What in the hell does one of your off-duty deputies have to do with this morning's double homicide?"

"We should discuss that back at the station." Tony stomped his way down the steps and reached them in three strides. Relief at feeling his solid presence beside her warred with the certainty that it would have been safer for both of them if he'd stayed on the porch. "There are circumstances—"

"We'll discuss it right here, and right now." Henderson rounded on Tony. "Half the town will hear about this on the six o'clock news, which means I need some answers to toss those roving vultures over there." He pointed to the reporters. "I want the truth, and if I can't get it from the two of you, I'll get Eric on the phone and see where that gets me."

"You'll have your answers," Tony said between clenched teeth. "Down at the station."

"And why not here, son? You got something in particular you need to hide from the good folks of this county?"

Angie could hear the nearby reporters scribbling in their notepads. Cameras zeroed in on them. Lacking any clear story to feed them, Henderson was making up his own headline—one shining the spotlight away from him and onto an even juicier target.

"Deputy Rivers isn't hiding anything, sir," she insisted.

Tony's raised hand kept her from continuing.

"Mayor Henderson, I'll give you and the chief whatever information you want, but it's not for public consumption." The tendons in Tony's neck corded. "Another teenage life is in danger. There are extenuating circumstances I haven't shared with the department yet."

"What other teenager?" Henderson had the good sense to modulate his tone for their ears only. "You've been stonewalling me since this morning, Officer Carter, and I've been put off for the last time! Tell me what the hell's going on, or—"

"My niece is the other teen," Tony bit out softly. "The men that were here today were after Maggie. And I don't think Sam Walker's through looking for her, just because I sent one of his guys to ICU."

"Your niece…" Henderson turned narrowed eyes to Angie. "The sheriff's daughter is mixed up in this drug mess, and I'm only hearing about it now?"

"There were extenuating circumstances, sir," Angie repeated.

"Hang your circumstances, Officer." For the first time, it was Henderson who scanned the milling crowd. He motioned them several feet away. "Tell me what's going on."

"At the department," Tony insisted.

"Deputy," the mayor huffed. "I'm done being patient. My ass is on the line with the press. I've got a town to placate, or I'll never win another election as long as I live—"

"This is about my family, Mayor Henderson, not your cushy office at city hall." Gone was the Tony who laughed off confrontation and moved on. In his place was a man who so closely resembled his imposing brother, it was all Angie could do not to take a step back right along with the mayor. "I couldn't care less if you can't get elected dog catcher. Someone is after my niece, and they're not going to get her. Not while I'm still breathing. So if you want to know what I know, then we're having this conversation in private."

The mayor's shock condensed into a hard-edged expression that promised Tony and Angie would be very sorry, very soon.

"Well, I'm not dog catcher yet, Deputy Rivers. Consider yourself suspended until further notice."

"You don't have the authority to do that." Angie grabbed at Tony's uninjured arm when he took a step toward the man.

"No?" Henderson countered. "Well, I know someone who does."

He motioned to the aide hovering nearby.

"Find Sheriff Rivers's cell number," he barked. "Get him on the phone. Now!"

When he turned back, it was to study first Angie, then the mere half inch separating her from Tony's solid presence. Not to mention her lingering hold on her deputy's arm.

Calculation filled the eyes that locked with hers.

"When I'm done speaking with your boss, Chief Carter, I'll meet you in your office." His eyes flicked to Tony. "Both of you. If you want to keep your jobs, don't even think about not playing it straight with me."

The mayor's aide tiptoed to a stop beside him, as if bracing for a coming explosion.

"We don't have the sheriff's number here, sir."

"Then get it!"

The mayor struck off toward the crowd of flash-bulbs and microphones at the end of the drive.

Angie dragged Tony farther away. "What the hell happened?"

A very unprofessional, un-chief-like part of her had come unglued as she'd listened helplessly through the phone to Tony's confrontation with the intruders. Then the connection had gone dead and she'd only gotten patchy information over the radio since.

Her raised hand almost touched the bandage near his shoulder. "The paramedic said the bullet only grazed you."

"I'm fine." Tony eased away, his attention trained over her shoulder at the audience they were no doubt attracting. "Sam Walker's the one who shot me."

"I heard. And if Walker was casing your house, that means—"

"This secret we've been keeping for my niece isn't a secret anymore," he finished for her.

He continued staring over her shoulder as the truth she'd already guessed sunk the rest of the way in.

"We have a leak in the department." She scanned the busy yard with him.

Her men were securing the scene and controlling the crowd. Everyone was busily going about doing the job. They made a great team. Her team.

Except one of them had set a nineteen-year-old girl up for an ambush.

"Here." She handed Tony the cell phone attached to her belt. "Call your brother. Get through to him before the mayor does, and tell Eric what he needs to know to bring Henderson to heel for a few hours."

The bewilderment etched on Tony's face matched her own shock. It was becoming too easy to put herself on the line for this man and what was important to him. His expression shifted to amazement, then something frighteningly intimate, considering half the department was roaming the yard around them.

"Helping me won't score you any points with Henderson." His voice was two octaves lower than its everyday timbre, exactly the way she remembered it from the other night at the Eight Ball.

"Forget scoring points." This was about protecting Maggie and ending this safely for everyone involved.

"What about the election?"

His concern washed over her. Filled up places

inside she'd gotten used to being empty. They'd talked about her deliberate choice to make the force her life. He hadn't pretended to understand everything, but he'd supported her like the best friend she'd needed.

Looking into his eyes now, she was certain she'd stumbled into far more than a best friend with Tony. And she was just as sure she didn't understand the first thing about what she needed anymore. It felt at that moment as if they were completely alone. And being alone with this man no longer came with the urge to slap herself senseless. That was the scariest realization of all.

In the midst of the damage she'd done to her future, and the danger Tony posed to the security she'd spent years fighting to capture, she felt strong instead of defeated. And just a little bit careless.

"Screw the election," she said, claiming out loud what had been chanting inside her for days. "If it means kowtowing to Henderson and not doing the job I know I should be doing, screw it!"

She had no back-up plan. Lissa was right. No new direction to pursue next, if the election didn't come off. But how was her *new* life supposed to work, when the truth was she was only hiding from her old one?

Tony's wayward smile rewarded her declaration. "You're the gutsiest woman I know, Chief Carter.

And considering the women in my family, that's saying something."

And suddenly the carelessness he so admired hardened into fear. Taking her obsession with her career off the menu was one thing. Ordering up a real life filled with the things she'd given up after Freddie's desertion was recklessness on a whole new level. Because the fantasy came complete with wanting to share everything with the surprisingly complicated man standing beside her.

A man who didn't have a clue how to love her in return.

"ERIC, LOOK AT THE CLOSET in this one. It's huge!"

Eric smiled at his wife's excitement. The picture in the real-estate brochure looked about the same as the others she'd shown him. But Carrinne had been brimming with excitement about their day of apartment shopping ever since they'd stepped off the plane.

She'd grabbed an armload of listings while Eric had pulled their luggage off the carousel. Then they'd hooked up with her friend, Jackie, who was their ride into the city. After a long lunch of catching up, they were finally on their way into the heart of Manhattan. The women had already worked through the bulk of the listings.

"There's no such thing as a huge closet in the

Village," Jackie quipped as she weaved through side streets toward their first must-see stop.

She'd been Carrinne's neighbor up until a year ago, before Carrinne had brought in a partner to share responsibilities at her accounting firm and moved herself and Maggie to Oakwood for the remainder of Eric's term. Carrinne had commuted back to New York often, whenever necessary for client meetings, which meant she and Jackie weren't totally out of touch. But there was still endless gossip to catch up on, not to mention shopping for ruinously expensive apartments that were so tiny, a walk-in closet was a cause for celebration.

It might not be a picture-perfect honeymoon by another man's standards. But watching his outrageously healthy wife's enthusiasm over their upcoming move back to the city she loved was the sweetest kind of foreplay for Eric.

"With what you'll be saving in airfare once you stop commuting, you should be able to afford as many closets as you want." He pulled his love of a lifetime closer. "Maybe even a separate one for your shoes."

Carrinne elbowed him as his hand caressed the underside of her breast. She snuggled closer. Her sigh tempted him to taste those teasing lips.

"The rent it'll take to store my shoes is nothing compared to garage fees for your motorcycle, and you haven't heard me complaining about bringing it along."

"Who's complaining? I love your sexy shoes." He smiled at the mental image of Carrinne tucked behind him on his bike, wearing leather pants and the pair of stiletto boots he'd bought her for Christmas. He ducked his head and nibbled the soft skin below her ear. "Hell, fill the bedroom with them, and I'll die a happy man."

"Stop that!" Her cheeks blushed pink.

Jackie chuckled from the front seat.

"You newlyweds think you can make it through the day, or should we head for my place and look at apartments later?" She slowed for the traffic that laid daily siege to the city. "Or maybe we should stop somewhere along the way, and get you guys a room."

"Just concern yourself with the lunatics on the road," Eric groused, burying his face in the silky strands of his bride's hair. "I'll have things under control back here before you know it."

Carrinne's devilish shriek was having a predictable effect on the anatomy behind his fly, when a cell phone chirped for attention.

"Oh!" She dived for her purse. "It's probably Maggie asking if she can have a sleepover. I told her she had to stay home this weekend and study for exams."

Eric checked his watch. "She's had about six hours to work on Tony. I'm betting she's charmed him into giving her anything she wants."

"It's not me," Carrinne said as the ringing continued.

With a grunt, Eric dug his phone out of his back pocket and checked the number of the incoming call.

"Angie said she'd get in touch if we tracked down the dealer who sold Travis the stuff that killed him."

Rubbing a finger across his wife's cheek, he flipped the phone open.

"Tell me something good."

"Eric." It was his brother instead of Angie. "You and Carrinne need to get back here."

"What's wrong?" His spine stiffened at the ragged tear in his brother's voice.

Carrinne grabbed his hand. Worry eclipsed the dreamy contentment that had softened her face seconds before. He squeezed her fingers.

"Tony?" he demanded. "Tell me what's wrong!"

MAGGIE PROPPED Max on her shoulder the way Nina had shown her, cotton cloth in place this time, then she patted his back. The watery hiccup that soon followed relieved her as much as it did the baby. He instantly stopped fussing.

She was still wearing the kid's breakfast, and it had been hours since her uncle had left to pick up a fresh change of clothes. She glanced at the clock again, but made herself look away and not freak the rest of the way out.

Nina and her great-grandfather were a few yards away at the main house, but Maggie had never felt more alone without her uncle there. Tony had agreed to help her. He'd taken her side, when she knew he thought it was a bad idea, even agreeing not to call her parents yet. Because she was family. Because he loved her.

So stop worrying, and wait for him to get back!

Tony had everything under control. Everything was going to be fine.

Yeah, right.

Claire was dead. How could anything be fine again?

She laid an almost-asleep-again Max back on the couch, peeled off the slimy burping thingie he'd drooled all over, and grabbed her cell phone from her backpack. She menued to her uncle's number. He should have at least called by now. A crisp knock at the front door sent the phone clattering to the floor.

She snatched it up and sank to the edge of the couch. She soothed the baby into a deeper sleep with numb fingers.

Stay away from the windows. Stay away from the doors, Tony had instructed in that no-nonsense way she wasn't used to yet. *No one can know you're here. Max's and your safety depends on it.*

Nina wouldn't have knocked, and she'd said it would be after dinner before she could come back over.

The ancient door creaked as someone jiggled the doorknob.

Maggie's heart clutched. Her uncle had seemed sure no one would come looking for her here. No one else but Angie and Nina knew she'd witnessed Claire's murder.

But just to be safe, don't answer the door. And don't call anyone.

Another knock had her picking Max up. Could she slip through the shadowy back door her uncle had made sure was locked? A wooded acre of land rimmed the edge of her great-grandfather's property. She could hide there, or slip around to the main house—

"Maggie Wilmington, are you in there?" a craggy, bossy voice demanded. "There's no point hiding. Calvin said he saw a youngster wandering the estate this morning, right before your uncle wanted to know if I'd seen you. And Nina's doing a lousy job of explaining why I saw her heading back to the house from out here."

Relieved, Maggie bolted toward the door and the familiar sound of her great-grandfather's voice. She unlocked the door at the same time that her cell phone rang.

Now her uncle was checking in.

"Perfect timing, hotshot," she said, answering the phone and swinging the door wide to the grumpy,

southern gentleman leaning on his signature black
cane. "Guess who just stopped by for a visit."

"Maggie, honey. Are you all right?"

The half angry, half terrified voice on the other
end of the phone wiped the sarcastic smile off
Maggie's face.

"Mom?" she croaked, turning her back on her
great-grandfather and scurrying back into the
cottage.

CHAPTER TEN

"Eric's booked on the next flight home, but it doesn't leave until morning. He can't make the connecting flight from Atlanta until then." Tony had sprawled in Angie's guest chair the second she'd shut the office door behind him. That is, the second after he'd dropped his department-issued firearm and badge onto her desk. Angie had carefully recorded the details of Maggie's statement about that morning's shootings, then she'd dispatched deputies to check out the shack Sam was supposedly using as a warehouse. Their next step was going over his own violent run-in with the man.

So far, he was holding it together. Playing it cool. Vintage Tony Rivers. Exactly what Angie needed him to be while she sorted out their mess. But something inside was going to explode if he didn't get back to his niece. Something unexpectedly humbled by the bond growing between them.

"What else did Eric say?" Angie asked.

"Not much. Just that you'd damn well better be at the airport at ten-thirty tomorrow when his plane lands. He's trying to talk Carrinne into staying in New York, but he isn't having much luck. She got Maggie on her cell phone while we were talking, so at least they heard firsthand that she was okay. They filled her in and told her to stay put until I get there."

"You're sure she's okay?"

"Maggie's fine." Tony stopped short of saying her great-grandfather was with her.

"Eric's seriously not going to take any more of the mayor's calls?"

"Not until he gets here and talks with you."

"Henderson's going to love that." Angie was pacing off her nervous energy. She hadn't pushed him to reveal where his niece was yet. But it was coming.

And so was his refusal to tell her.

He'd trust Angie with his life, and with Maggie's. But that trust no longer extended to the rest of the department. Which meant Maggie had to stay hidden. And it was best for Angie if she didn't know where. He'd already done enough damage to her relationship with the mayor.

"Henderson did get through to Eric once, right after I did." Tony added. "My brother told him to work it out with you until he got home. That you're in charge of the department. Then he called me back to say the same thing. He's backing you all the way."

"At least for the next twenty hours or so, until he gets home. Which is about how long I'll have a job."

"No one's taking your job away."

The look she shot him said she didn't know whether to laugh or throw something at his head. "Yeah, that's why Eric's tripped all over himself to contact me personally."

"He's got Carrinne on his hands. Travel plans to make."

"He's got a lot to say to me, and he wants to do it in person."

"That's just Eric."

"He knows about us, doesn't he?"

Tony didn't answer, but he didn't look away either.

"Well," she said. "That adds a whole new dimension to things, doesn't it?"

"Like any of this is your fault." Tony pushed out of the chair before she could trudge back to the other side of the room.

"No. It's *your* fault." Her miserable smile blew away his decision to keep his hands off.

She leaned into his touch, when she should have been furious. Ran a tentative finger across the bandage covering the flesh wound he'd already forgotten about.

"But I knew what I was doing when I kissed you the other night," she confessed. "It was my choice to back you up with the mayor. And I'd do it again, if it meant keeping Maggie, that baby or any other kid in this town safe."

"I… Damn, Angie…" His fingers tangled in hair that somewhere between his house and the station had lost the clip that normally held it back. Softness invited him to linger. Like he needed an excuse. She'd already surprised him in a million different ways, and something told him he'd only scratched the surface. "I shouldn't be here, touching you. But I… It's like I've been speeding out of control for months, ever since Eric decided to move to New York. And now Maggie's in trouble. And for some reason…"

"For some reason," she continued when he couldn't, "us and out of control go together a little too well, don't we?"

"What happened to keeping things safe and by the book?"

"You," she said, erasing his last easy way out. "And me. And my newfound respect for how good careless can feel."

"I said I'd get out of your way, Angie." He'd never forgive himself if he became another regret she had to fight to put behind her. "What about your career? The election? Your chance at sheriff—"

"My chance is gone." She sounded like she had it all figured out. "Maybe it was, even before things with you and Maggie got so off track. I guess there are limits to what I'm willing to sacrifice for the job, after all. I'm not up for the mayor's politics. Not anymore. So, I'm done."

She flashed that impish grin, the one that could own a part of his soul if he let it. A soul he'd thought long immune to any relationship he couldn't walk away from.

She made him wish he had the guts to tell her all the things she made him feel, and the reasons he'd never let himself feel them for any other woman. Only this wasn't the time or the place.

Hell, there wasn't going to be a time or place. Not for them.

There was no *them!*

As if in agreement, Angie inched away and headed for her desk. She picked up a file from the clutter of paperwork.

"Forget the election," she said. "We've got bigger problems."

"Don't do that." He laid his hands on the edge of the desk, suddenly spoiling for a fight.

"What?"

"Don't act like losing the sheriff's spot is no big deal. I know what you've given up to get here. How hard you've busted your ass. What you're trying to put behind you. This job means everything to you. And I'm not going to let you—"

"It doesn't mean everything!" She threw the papers down. She wouldn't meet his gaze. "Call me crazy, but I finally care more about making my life better than being sheriff. So save yourself the guilt trip and the misplaced responsibility, Rivers. This is about a whole lot more than just you."

"Angie, I'm…" He was an ass. And she didn't owe him a thing. "Look—"

"Is she safe?"

"What? Who?"

"Maggie—your niece?" Still no eye contact. "Carrinne's talked with her. Is she all right?"

"Maggie's fine." His mind flashed to an image of what could have happened if it had been Maggie those two goons had stumbled across at his house.

"But you're not going to tell me where she is, are you?"

Angie finally stared him down, her warrior's spirit claiming his admiration and a little more of his heart with each passing second. After Freddie Peters had finished with her, she'd been so sure she wasn't the kind of woman men built their lives around. It made Tony sick, the way she believed she wasn't good enough and never would be for any man.

Not for the first time, he wanted to hunt down her now happily married ex and have a very up-close and personal, man-to-man conversation. More than that, he wished he had it in him to prove to Angie how wrong her fiancé had been.

"Maggie's in a safe place," he said instead. "And the less you know about where, the better. I'm already on suspension. Let me take the heat."

An efficient nod, and she was once again studying the file on the desk.

"There was no gun." Her finger stalled on its track down the top page of the report.

"What?"

"The man you shot at the house," she continued, still reading. "You said he was carrying a gun, but none was found at the scene."

It was like having a bucket of freezing water thrown in his face.

"The… He waved it in my face. In my niece's room! When I grabbed him, Sam shot at me…." Tony rubbed where the bullet had nicked his arm. "I fell while I returned fire. I must have blacked out for a few seconds. By the time I got back on my feet, the other guy was bleeding like a sonovabitch, and Walker was long gone."

"According to the on-site team, there was no gun," she said, her game face on when she finally looked up. "We're waiting on the test results on his hands to confirm if he actually fired a weapon."

"He had a gun, Angie. He turned it on me. I had no choice but to shoot."

The office door swung inward without a knock of warning.

"The physical evidence seems to suggest otherwise." Mayor Henderson didn't stop moving until he stood between Tony and Angie. He held a copy of the hastily prepared field report in his hand.

The overweight man, who had a camera-ready smile for every handshake and baby kiss, wore an enormous frown at the moment.

"That puts your story on a somewhat precarious footing, son, even with your brother covering your ass all the way from New York. So why don't we get down to the truth. Those boys were after something at your house, Rivers. Drugs maybe? Is that your connection to this morning's shooting? You've got yourself mixed up in all this, and now your family's a target?"

Tony held his tongue, his gaze warning Angie away from protecting him. Henderson was gunning for a public whipping boy, and Tony had stepped to the front of the line. If she wasn't careful, axing her run for sheriff wouldn't be the only thing on the mayor's agenda.

"Deputy Rivers being involved in drugs is a ridiculous assumption." Angie crossed her arms and faced off against the mayor, not backing down for a second.

Tony didn't know which to do first—kiss her or shake some sense into her.

"As ridiculous as you not at least allowing for the possibility, after today's events," the mayor countered. "Drugs are rampant in my town. People are being killed. And as far as I can see, this department's done nothing about it. Could that be because someone around here doesn't want to see the scum dealing the stuff stopped?"

"There's nothing I'd love better—" Tony started to say.

"Or could it be," Angie interrupted, "that your city council hasn't forked over enough funding to stop one of the church's potluck dinners, let alone drug trafficking. We need twice as much manpower. My deputies are ready to put in the overtime, but your council refuses to approve the extra hours. We need state-of-the-art surveillance equipment, but you've kept a stranglehold on our budget for six months. And don't get me started on your homespun interference, every time one of my deputies questions someone related to one of your cronies. If you'd only let us do our job months ago—"

"Your job is to catch the criminals bringing this trash

into town." The mayor pointed a finger at the woman he'd championed until that morning. "Not harassing decent folks to cover your incompetence. Meanwhile someone in your department, by your own admission, is passing information along to the people you're supposed to be stopping. Or did I misunderstand? Is there or is there not a leak?"

"Yes, sir." Tony rode out the impulse to throw something other than protocol at the man. "We have a leak."

"But you're not it, huh? And I'm supposed to believe you, after you tell me the scum who killed a runaway teen this morning showed up at your place a few hours ago for round two. And on top of that, somehow your niece is mixed up in this mess?"

"Tony's not our leak," Angie said. "He's kept me in the loop with everything he knows about this morning's homicides."

"Then why am I only hearing about this now?" The mayor's fist pounded the edge of the desk.

"Because I wasn't at liberty to relay the information."

"Or could it be because you were covering your boyfriend's ass!"

The commotion on the other side of Angie's office door died to a whisper at the mayor's thunderous accusation.

"Don't think I haven't heard the rumors," the man

continued. "And don't think because you're the sheriff's kid brother and friend, that the two of you can get it on and there won't be hell to pay when the rest of this is cleared up."

"That's enough!" Tony clenched his fists.

"I couldn't agree more." The mayor's finger shot in Angie's direction. "You covered for him back at the house. And considering your personal relationship with the good deputy here, it's not a far stretch that you've been covering for him all day. Maybe even longer."

"No sir, I've been doing my job. We have an eyewitness to this morning's shooting, and the girl was on the run. It was my decision that as few people as possible were to know about Maggie, until we had her safely in-house. I detailed Deputy Rivers to secure our witness, because of his access to his niece. Totally within the discretion of my command. Totally by the book."

Except the woman had left the book behind hours ago, and both she and Tony knew it.

"Maggie Rivers witnessed Walker kill Claire Morton and that other guy?" Some of the steam fizzled from Henderson's tirade.

"Yes," Tony confirmed. "My niece was there, and I've been trying to persuade her to come in for her own protection, and to make an official statement ever since."

"Persuade!" The man actually sputtered. "She's a teenager. You don't persuade. You haul her ass in here, and let her parents worry about whether or not you've hurt the girl's feelings. This is a homicide investigation, son."

"There's a baby involved, sir." Angie didn't blink as she stuck her neck out another reckless inch. "And Ms. Rivers threatened to leave town. She's determined to find the child's out-of-town grandparents."

"What child?"

"Claire Morton's son," Tony added. "My niece has been taking care of him since this morning."

"You…" The mayor rubbed a hand over his eyes. "You mean to tell me, you're not only hiding a witness to an ongoing investigation, but you're harboring a baby no one knew about, whose mother is lying on a slab down at the morgue?"

"Yes, sir," Angie said. "It was essential that no one knew about the baby, or Sam Walker might make the connection to Maggie, and from there to her witnessing this morning's shootings. When Walker ultimately did, he came looking for her. She's hidden at a safe house now, so there's no more risk to her or the baby."

The mayor smiled like they were old friends. The man's eyes promised retribution. "Let me get this straight. I have another shooting victim in E.R.

because you used your *discretion* to hide a girl who'd snatched her friend's baby, instead of turning the kid over and bringing the girl in for questioning? And now you're covering for your boyfriend here, by spouting department protocol and calling wherever you've stashed her a *safe house?*"

"Maggie's testimony is critical." Angie's words all but steamed. "I made sure she stayed in Oakwood until she would talk."

"And has she talked?"

"Yes, sir. Deputy Rivers took her statement. She overheard enough this morning to make a case against Walker once we have him in custody. Information that may be key in prosecuting him. Information I don't currently intend to share outside of essential personnel."

"Because of this leak?"

"Yes, sir."

"The same leak that sent those two thugs to your house while you were off duty?" he directed at Tony. "Where one of them happened to stumble into your gun?"

"Yes, sir." Tony followed Angie's lead, not that he expected it to do any good. "I was on the phone with Chief Carter when they showed up. We were making final plans to bring Maggie in—"

"Isn't that convenient." Henderson looked less

than blown away. "A neat and tidy explanation for some shady conduct by both you and your boy here."

"*Deputy* Rivers is not my boy. And I seriously doubt he finds anything convenient about his niece being in danger."

If she was expecting embarrassment, the mayor wasn't playing along.

"Where is she?" he demanded.

"Who?" Tony pretended not to understand.

"Maggie Rivers! Where is this departmental *safe house* you've invented? Since the two of you seem so determined to stonewall me, maybe I should call your brother to get some answers?"

"You could try, I suppose." Tony took his time sitting in the guest chair and stretching his legs in front of him. "But I doubt Eric's going to be in any bigger hurry to put his daughter at risk than I am. There aren't going to be any more leaks from this department, not where Maggie is concerned. She's safe. No one in town but me, not even Chief Carter, knows where she is. And Maggie's not moving an inch until we have Sam Walker behind bars."

"Too bad," Henderson added mildly. "Since she's your only corroboration that Walker is the shooter that killed Claire Morton."

"What are you talking about?" Angie asked.

"Where's your evidence that Sam and the man

Deputy Rivers shot were at his house uninvited? Without the girl to back Rivers, your case kind of falls apart, doesn't it?"

Tony swallowed. "That's one way of looking at it."

"Maybe Maggie would point the finger at you, instead of Sam Walker. Maybe it's you the man was after, because you killed his girlfriend and associate this morning? Or maybe he got wind you were trying to frame him for the job?"

CHAPTER ELEVEN

"THAT'S NOT WHAT HAPPENED," Angie insisted.

"Do you have the ballistics back from this morning?" the mayor demanded without looking away from Tony.

She hesitated. "Not yet."

"I'm assuming you put a rush on them."

"Of course."

"Of course," the politician mimicked. "Unless you don't want them hurried along for some reason. Where were you this morning, Deputy Rivers, around the time of the shootings?"

"At home." Tony closed his eyes briefly. "Alone."

"Nowhere near the apartment where Claire Morton was killed," Angie quickly added. Tony had just graduated from scapegoat to prime suspect. "He's not our inside man, Mayor Henderson."

"It's as good an explanation as any I've heard. Now if he'd see fit to produce his niece—"

"That's not going to happen," Tony said.

"Well until it does, you remain on suspension." Henderson looked Tony up and down. "The only reason I can see not to have you locked up for obstruction now is that you're the only link we have to the girl. Cooperate from here on out, and you might clear your name. Keep acting like you've got something to hide, and I'll have your butt in jail, and I don't care who your big brother and your girlfriend are!"

The mayor and his considerable girth exited without another glance at Angie, who was technically the only person with the authority to carry through on the man's threats. But this was a small town. And small-town governments moved at their own pace. Oakwood's seemed to be peddling backward with each passing second.

It wouldn't take much for the city council to suspend her as chief and acting sheriff, and replace her with someone the mayor could better control. Eric, too, for that matter, even though his popularity would be more of an obstacle.

"Tony." She walked around her desk and closed the door. "Don't wor—"

He shot out of his chair, sending it skidding away. "Stay away from me, Ange. I'm poison in the mayor's eyes. You don't want to be anywhere near me until this is over."

"There's nowhere else for me to be but near you.

As far as the mayor's concerned, we're already so close we should be wearing matching jackets with big red bull's-eyes on them." She worked hard for sarcasm. Tony had been throwing up walls between them since Henderson's arrival at the house. "You can't keep winging this on your own. You were almost killed this afternoon. You've got to trust me."

"Damn it. This isn't about trust. The mayor's out for my badge. Stand too close and he'll have yours, too."

"Then he can have it! You've been protecting your family. No one can blame you for that. I'm not bailing, whether you want my help or not."

"Want your help... Angie, I'm trying to protect you. I've broken I don't know how many departmental regulations, and you don't want any part of that."

"So what's your next step, if you're so determined to do this on your own?"

Tony rocked backward.

"That's exactly what I said to Maggie this morning." His shrug was a shadow of its former, irreverent self. "There is nothing next. I'm keeping my niece safe until her mama and daddy get back. Everyone will be fine, life will get back to normal, and by the end of the summer they'll all head for New York."

It sounded easy enough. No big deal. Only Angie knew just how hard it was for him to watch his family move away.

"Tony, you aren't in this alone." She watched his dark eyes melt to that amazing shade of cocoa she saw in her dreams.

He was right, she should walk. Her hand rose to his chest instead, same as it had at the Eight Ball. Careless? Oh yeah. But she couldn't help herself.

"I've got your back for as long as you need me," she promised.

"Not an enviable location these days, darlin'." His use of the endearment while they were in the office was riskier than her touch. And sexy beyond belief.

Something about Tony had changed during the confrontation with the mayor. If he'd ever given a damn about protocol and regulations, he was over it. As if to prove her point, he leaned closer, the lips she'd been staring at brushing across her cheek. He made her feel reckless. All woman.

"I swear, Angie." His deep voice caressed her ear. "There's no one in this town I'd rather have in my corner right now. Tell yourself you're not woman enough for a man because you can't have kids. Hide in your uniform and your career, if that's what gets you through the day. But, darlin', you're more woman than this SOB would be lucky to handle in a lifetime."

"Tony…"

She pushed at his chest, but there was no real

effort behind it. Then she was pulling him closer, her lips sighing against his, because the truth was she'd die if he didn't kiss her back.

Thank heavens, he was more than happy to oblige.

He groaned into her mouth, his large hands sliding in an arch of mischief to cup her backside. He pulled her against him, allowing her to explore the strong line of his neck with her lips and tongue. Snuggle closer to his arousal. He rewarded her with a sinful growl that had no business making an appearance at work.

But damn if he didn't feel good. Every bad-boy inch of him. And he wanted her just as much as she wanted him, as much as she'd wanted him two nights ago when she'd said this could never happen again. He needed to go, he needed to focus on his niece. But for once the town's most accomplished playboy seemed incapable of walking away.

"You—" One more kiss, and she inched away. "You should go, Deputy."

"Technically, I'm not your deputy anymore." Breathing hard, he pecked a kiss on the freckles sprinkled across her nose. Those chocolate-brown eyes simmered, even as they twinkled. "The mayor just fired my ass."

"Suspended," she corrected.

"Whatever." His shrug confirmed he didn't care.

Smiling in spite of herself, she returned to her desk.

"You need to get back to Maggie," she said, doing what she did best. Taking care of business.

Nodding, Tony headed for the door, plucking the bag of clothes he'd nabbed for himself and Maggie before driving into the station.

"What about our leak?" she asked.

"I think we both know where to start looking." He shook his head at the idea of a man they'd both ridden with working for dope dealers. But only two people had been privy to the details of this morning's shootings, and only one of them had had a burr up his ass about the department for months. "The question is, what are we going to do about it? How do we stop him and Sam Walker at the same time?"

"We'll think of something. I'll call Eric and get his input." Might as well face the music before the sheriff got back in town. "I'll keep hunting down Claire's parents. You stay focused on Maggie tonight. You're armed, right?"

Tony glanced at his department-issued weapon lying useless on her desk.

"You bet your sweet ass I am," he said with a wink.

But his smile had faded into a concerned frown by the time he opened the office door and walked out.

Damn straight she had his back.

SHUTTING DOWN THE HEAT shimmering through her from Tony's kiss, Angie stomped out of her office.

...darlin', you're more woman than this SOB would be lucky to handle in a lifetime....

And strangely enough, given the high-stakes game they were playing with Sam Walker, for the first time in a long time she actually felt like the woman Tony saw inside her.

They'd both lost their minds.

"Deputy Rhodes, I'd like to see you in my office," Angie bit out. "You and Tyler both."

"I'm not sure Buddy's here anymore." Martin remained seated at his desk, typing up a report displayed on his computer monitor. "That new wife of his gets real prickly when the man's not home in time for his supper."

"He hasn't clocked out yet." Angie glanced toward the time cards. "I suggest you find him, print out both your reports, and get your butts in my office, pronto. Details from this morning's homicide were leaked."

"You mean the part about there being a baby there during the shooting, and someone maybe running off with the kid?" Rhodes lifted an eyebrow. "I thought you wanted that kept under wraps."

"I did." The man had balls, she had to give him

that. "And because it wasn't, two thugs took potshots at Tony this afternoon."

"Because Maggie's got her friend's baby stashed somewhere, and Sam Walker thinks she heard something she shouldn't have this morning?" When Angie didn't answer, Rhodes dropped his pen to his desk. "That's what's been buzzing around the station since the shooting at the Rivers place. It's the only thing that makes sense."

"Yes, Maggie's involved, and Sam's figured it out. And I want to know how any of this was leaked in the first place."

"Yeah?" The smirk she despised was in rare form as Rhodes raised his ex-jock self out of his chair. "Didn't look like the mayor was all too happy 'bout things himself, when he came charging out after talking with you and Tony. His kid made the mistake of asking what was wrong, and the man nearly bit Garret's head off. Rumor has it, Eric's flying back in the morning to clean everything up for you."

Rhodes's tone broadcast his appreciation of the mess the department had dissolved into after only one day of Angie's solo leadership. Almost as if he wouldn't mind helping things along.

"In my office, Deputy. Five minutes."

"Yes, ma'am." He ambled away at a snail's pace. The man and his snide, backhanded comments were a daily annoyance. But did he really have it in him to send armed men to his friend's house to gun down a nineteen-year-old girl?

He'd ridden shifts with Tony most of the last two years. They were weekend buddies who played pickup football in the park. Rhodes, as much a member of the town's bachelors' club as Tony, ate dinner at the Rivers house at least once a month. He teased Maggie into hysterics each time she stopped by the station. He was an ass, but was he really capable of screwing over his friend and colleagues, not to mention the youth of this town, by backing the local drug lord?

Martin couldn't really be their leak.

Could he?

CHAPTER TWELVE

"HOW DARE YOU NOT INFORM ME that my great-grand-daughter's life is in danger!" Old Man Wilmington sputtered as soon as Tony entered the overseer's cottage. "And you left her here, all by herself, while you got yourself shot at by the men you're hiding her from?"

Tony shut the door behind himself, having spent the better part of a half hour making the ten-minute drive over from the station, carefully guaranteeing, as he wound through late-afternoon traffic in a haphazard pattern, that he wasn't being followed. Carefully not thinking about how much he wanted Angie Carter back in his arms.

"Where's Maggie?" He needed to see for himself that the ugliness back at the house hadn't touched his niece.

It didn't matter that Eric and Carrinne had both said she was fine. Believing bad things couldn't happen to people he cared about wasn't high on the list of things Tony was good at.

"She's asleep in one of the bedrooms." Wilmington nodded to the half-closed door of one of the rooms behind him. "Nina dropped off fresh towels and sheets earlier. Maggie was upset when she heard about the altercation at your house, but her parents calmed her down. She'd worked herself into an exhausted heap, so I sent her and the baby off to bed."

While the man talked, Tony crossed to the bedroom. A touch from behind, directly on the ill-fitting bandage throbbing on his upper arm, had Tony spinning around. "Son of a bitch!"

Wilmington jerked his hand away. Shock shadowed the sunken angles of his cheeks. He studied the blood spatters on the wrap covering Tony's shoulder.

"My granddaughter said you'd been injured."

"I'm fine." Tony peeked into the darkened bedroom. The quaking inside him eased at the sight of his niece sprawled across the bed, her breathing the heavy and even rhythm of deep sleep. The baby dozed beside her.

Maggie was safe.

And by God, she was going to stay that way.

"I demand to know what's going on," the old man said behind him. "I haven't spoken to anyone in town, because my granddaughter asked me not to. Is it true that it's not even safe for Maggie to go into the department? And why is it that I had to figure all of this out for myself? My housekeeper told me nothing, even though I pay her a king's ransom to do as I say. It took me an hour, once I figured all Nina's coming and going had something to do with you looking for your niece, before the woman would tell me where my great-granddaughter was!"

"You should give her a raise." Tony closed the bedroom door to a crack. "If it wasn't for Nina, Maggie would have kept running this morning."

Wilmington settled himself in one of the overstuffed chairs beside the couch and set his cane aside. "That baby I understand belongs to one of Maggie's friends. A young girl that's now dead?"

"Yes." Tony wouldn't have chosen to have Wilmington in the loop, but the events of the day had been out of his hands from the start. Why should this be any different? "The man who killed her is now after Maggie."

"The same man who did that to you?" Wilmington pointed to Tony's shoulder.

"Yes."

That earned him several seconds of silence.

"Then I'm glad I insisted on staying and watching over my great-granddaughter until you returned."

It wasn't the same as saying he was glad Tony was

okay, but Tony couldn't help but warm to someone as committed as he was to protecting Maggie.

"I'm sure Carrinne was relieved to know you were here," he said.

Wilmington had once told Maggie's teenage mother to have an abortion or leave his house. Now he was a doting great-grandfather.

"I'll do whatever it takes to ensure the child's safety."

Whatever it takes.

The man had been a nemesis to the Rivers family since the dawn of time, but he was growing on Tony by the second.

"How hidden is this place?" he asked, his wave encompassing the tightly drawn shades blotting out the lavender shadows of dusk. Had he really been down at the station that long?

"It's been here for at least fifty years. It's not even noted on the county tax records, for which I'm grateful every quarter when I pay through the nose for the privilege of owning real estate inside the city limits. No one's lived here for several decades, though I think your brother and Carrinne might have met out here once or twice. I have Nina tidy up a couple of times a month. Don't ask me why. I should have torn it down ages ago."

From the decay cloaking everything from the sagging furniture to the faded pictures on the walls,

Tony was a little surprised it hadn't fallen down on its own.

"So if someone came looking for Maggie, thinking she might be with you," Tony reasoned, "they'd probably stop looking at the main house?"

Wilmington's faded blue eyes sparked. He nodded.

"As long as no one sees me or anyone else walking back and forth from this run-down shack," the older man added.

"My thoughts exactly."

"You planning on heading anywhere else tonight?"

"A bomb couldn't budge me until my brother gets off that plane in the morning." From the waistband of his jeans, Tony withdrew the Beretta he'd retrieved from the house. His personal weapon outside of the job. Placing it on the rickety coffee table, he added, "No one's getting close enough to even breathe the same air as my niece."

Wilmington's expression hardened. He looked ready to take a shot at Sam Walker himself. Maybe the man really *had* grown to care deeply for his family over the last year.

It wasn't any harder to believe than Tony understanding too little, too late just how lonely his calculated solitude could feel. Warmth filled him at the memory of Angie's fierce expression when she'd promised to guard his back for as long as he needed her. The woman made him want things he'd been determined not to miss in his life.

"Then I best head back to the house and make sure my alarm system's set," Wilmington said. "Everyone but Nina should be gone by now. I'll let her know you're back."

"I'm sure Maggie would love to have you here in the morning, while we wait for her parents," Tony offered.

Wilmington nodded thoughtfully. The novelty of a Rivers inviting a Wilmington for a visit wasn't lost on the older man.

"I'll be here," he said. "My great-granddaughter needs her family around her right now."

"Then I'll let Chief Carter know you're onboard. Oh, and do us all a favor. If your friend the mayor comes sniffing around for details, steer clear of the man. Henderson has it in for me because I won't produce Maggie fast enough to suit him, and Angie doesn't need any more trouble."

"The chief's helping you thumb your nose at the mayor?" Wilmington's bemused grin softened the lines creasing his face. "She's helping you hide Maggie from him?"

"Let's say the man's not taking kindly to being kept out of the loop."

"No, I wouldn't expect he would be." Wilmington cleared his throat. "And if I know Henderson, he's holding your job and Deputy Carter's election over your heads to get what he wants?"

It was a rhetorical question. Tony didn't waste his time answering.

He hated what backing him was costing Angie. Almost as much as he hated her willingness to sacrifice the sheriff's position she'd fought so hard to win. Her family accused her of not caring about anything but her job. They couldn't be more wrong. And being one of the things Angie cared about didn't sit well with him. At least it shouldn't.

"I'll be back in the morning." Wilmington opened the faded front door. "Tell your Chief Carter not to worry too much about the mayor. There are tons of skeletons in the man's closet, and I know just how to use them."

His Chief Carter.

What did he have, really? A job he'd just been suspended from? A family that was leaving in a little over a month? A player lifestyle he'd once thrived on that now felt as empty as the threadbare living room closing in around him?

Angie Carter wasn't *Tony's* anything, and he'd damn well better remember it.

"THEN WE'RE AGREED," Angie said to Eric over the phone after she'd finished with deputies Rhodes and

Tyler. "We don't have a choice, if we're going to flush out the leak and corner Walker while keeping Maggie out of it."

The reports from this morning still cluttered her desk. She scoured them for details she might have missed.

"I don't like the timing," her sheriff growled quietly. "We don't want to rush, misfire and lose our chance."

Angie could picture Carrinne hanging on every word her husband said. Eric was keeping his end of the conversation as low-key as possible, so he didn't scare his wife more. So far, that had saved Angie from the balling out she knew she deserved for not calling him first thing that morning.

"It's absolutely the right time," she reasoned. "We're running Sam to the ground, now that we know where he stores the stuff. You wouldn't believe the quantity of meth we're pulling out of that shack— raw materials and finished product. His network is officially shut down, thanks to Maggie's information and the equipment we've confiscated. Sam has to be gunning to finish this. If the plan works, we can have him and our leak out of the picture, and get Maggie in the clear, by tomorrow afternoon."

"Everyone's out beating the bushes?" Eric asked.

"Whatever we can do to keep Walker on edge."

The deputies who weren't tossing Sam's storage unit were tightening the screws on every source and snitch in town. The department had the upper hand and the momentum they'd lacked before. There would be no soft place for Sam Walker to land tonight. Only chaos and disarray. The jail was filling up fast, some of the surprising faces behind bars familiar, we-go-way-back friends no one would have suspected. "I guarantee, Sam'll be mad as hell by tomorrow morning."

"Don't overdo it. We don't want to piss the guy off to the point that he does something reckless."

"I doubt he's stupid enough to try anything tonight, not after Tony took out his man at your house. He'll wait it out and regroup."

"So he can do something stupid tomorrow, instead?" Eric bit out.

"You got it." Angie smiled in spite of the seriousness of the topic. "I've got you covered at the department, and Tony's with Maggie. Everything's in place."

"My brother would die himself, before he'd let something happen to my daughter. He's as over losing people he loves as I am." Eric's words were thick with pride and the deeper emotions that came with talking about his and Tony's past.

"Yes, he is." Angie's heart hurt at the thought of Tony guarding his niece alone tonight. Facing how easily they could have lost her along with Claire. And there'd be no one there to ease the emotional fallout, which was exactly the way Tony insisted he wanted things. "So, we're a go, then? I'll set up the sting and get everyone in position, and you'll be our ace in the hole when we spring the trap."

"You really think it could be Martin Rhodes?" The jagged edge of Eric's voice caught at her heart rate. "Damn, Angie, the man's a family friend."

"We don't know anything for sure. It's only a hunch. But he's been gunning for me for years, and he thinks I don't have the smarts to find my own butt when I need to wipe it. If he's not our guy, I'm betting he won't be able to keep his mouth shut about my plan once I brief him and Buddy in the morning. Let him complain and tell the rest of the department how stupid I am. Either way, word will get out. We'll nail our bastard."

"Then we wait," Eric agreed with a sigh.

"Why don't I give Tony a call over at the Wilmington place," she offered mildly. It was a wild guess, but she was getting good at guessing what Tony had going on underneath those glorious good looks. "I'll catch him up on everything, so you don't have to talk about it anymore with Carrinne there."

"Call his cell," Eric agreed, confirming without realizing it that Tony had Maggie stashed somewhere on the Wilmington property. "I'm not even sure the overseer's place has a phone. Let's get this done, Angie. No more surprises. No more risky choices."

Her phone chirped over his subtle reprimand of the risks she'd already taken with his department and his family. Not to mention whatever he knew of her personal involvement with his brother. The memory of Tony kissing her, then her reaching for more, had her checking the phone's display.

"It's the mayor again." And who would have guessed she'd feel relieved by that? "You still want me to take the lead there?"

"You're in charge," Eric said without a second's hesitation. Empowering her, even though he had every reason to be angry. They'd talk more, she was sure, but she still had his confidence, same as she had from day one out of the academy.

"Thanks, Sheriff."

"You bet." Encouragement filled his voice. "I'll see you soon."

"Yes, sir."

Swallowing the unexpected tightness in her throat, she pressed the button for the other line.

"Carter here."

"Looks like you have connections in high places after all," Henderson said, not bothering with preliminaries.

"I don't know what you're talking about, sir. The only person I've spoken to is Sheriff Rivers, and—"

"Oliver Wilmington just phoned, that's what I'm talking about. He suggests that I cut you and Deputy Rivers some slack. In fact, the old goat downright insisted. A Wilmington going to bat for a Rivers. I never thought I'd see that day."

Neither had anyone else in Oakwood, Angie was certain. What had Tony been up to?

"Too bad Mr. Wilmington wasn't at the hospital a few minutes ago to bully Deputy Rivers's shooting victim into cooperating," Henderson continued.

"What? Why?"

"I thought for sure you'd heard by now, what with you being in charge and all."

"My focus has been on getting Sam Walker and the rest of his gang into custody." Angie clicked her e-mail in-box and scanned for updates, ignoring the mayor's attitude and his earlier threat to block her election.

It was a relief, actually, not to give a damn what Henderson thought for a change.

"Then let me be the bearer of bad tidings. The man Deputy Rivers gunned down in his home died thirty minutes ago. He never regained consciousness to deny or confirm Rivers's story of what happened."

Angie allowed her stunned silence to last for all of a second. Grabbing the reports from Tony's shooting, she flipped through them.

"I'm looking at that paperwork now, sir." Pictures illustrating body positions and bullet trajectories. Detailed descriptions of the fallen man's movements and the exact location of his body when her team had arrived. Tony's statement about the struggle, about Sam Walker firing the first shot, then Tony returning fire. "Everything seems to be in order. The evidence is straightforward. There's no reason to doubt Tony's account."

"Except thanks to Deputy Rivers's expertise with his gun, there's no other witness, just like this morning. Not unless you produce Maggie Rivers or nail Sam Walker—assuming the man would be gracious enough to give Mr. Rivers an alibi. Short of that, I'm afraid I have to insist on an internal investigation. Which means, whether Rivers follows orders and brings his niece in or not, he stays on suspension until the matter is resolved."

"Deputy Rivers was doing his job—"

"He was off duty, and he killed a man under suspicious circumstances, after hiding a relative's alleged involvement in an earlier homicide."

"He's a good cop."

"Then what's he doing hiding a key witness and

a baby he has no business keeping? Has he told you where the girl is?"

Angie forced her next words to ring with conviction.

"No sir, I have no idea where he or Maggie Rivers are at the moment."

Instinct, not regulations, was the only way to fight this battle. Relying on anything else would put the people she was protecting at even more risk. Her by-the-book days, she realized, had officially come to an end.

"Now why don't I believe you?" the mayor asked. "I've called an emergency city council session for tomorrow afternoon. You're lucky we can't meet first thing in the morning on a Sunday. As it is, you have a little time to come to your senses. Pull yourself together, Ms. Carter. Or Oakwood will find itself another chief deputy who knows how to put the job before her personal life."

CHAPTER THIRTEEN

TONY DREW HIS GUN. His gaze shifted to the bedroom where Maggie and the baby were still cuddled together. He pressed himself against the wall beside the front door and waited for whoever was outside to make the first move.

He'd been listening to the old shack creak for hours, ignoring the rest of the world as it slipped from dusk into the darkness of night. A cup of coffee in hand, made on an ancient stove with the fresh groceries Nina had produced when she'd sneaked back one last time, he'd had plenty enough to do. Contemplating his new position as the mayor's prime suspect in not one but two drug-related shootings, for starters.

Anything but letting his mind wander in Angie Carter's direction. Anything but facing his messed-up life choices, not to mention the nightmares of the past lurking way too close for him to sleep tonight.

Then the new creak had come. The one out of place with the sound of the shack settling around him.

Someone was walking up the dilapidated porch.

The almost golden illumination from the only two lamps in the living room cast anorexic pools of light that didn't reach the shadows where he stood by the door. Footsteps drew closer, near soundless in the self-conscious way of someone trying hard not to be heard. Another creak.

Sam Walker had found them.

Tony raised his gun, then hesitated.

There was a chance it was Old Man Wilmington again. It could even be Nina.

Damn it!

He positioned himself between the door and the bedroom where his niece slept, and raised his weapon to chest level.

"Whoever's out there, announce yourself and step the hell away from the door! I'm armed, and you're trespassing."

"Tony?" the last voice he'd expected whispered back.

"Angie?"

He shoved the gun into his belt and turned the dead bolt. Angie slipped through the door, shutting it quickly so no light escaped into the darkness beyond.

"What the hell are you doing here?" he barked. One glimpse of her and he was clenching his hands to keep them to himself. "Why didn't you call first? I could have blown your head off!"

"And give you the chance to talk me out of coming? I wasn't followed, relax. I came in my truck, and I parked out of sight almost a mile away."

Relax?

Sure. Forget that having her standing there had chased away the darkness folding in on him. Forget that he wanted to beg her not to leave again.

Relax.

"How did you even know where we were?"

"I guessed, while I was on the phone with your brother. Eric confirmed it without even knowing. Then the mayor called—"

"Henderson knows we're here!"

"Of course not." She unhooked her gun belt. Laid it on the ancient *Life* magazines on the table and looked around. "Where are the kids?"

"In the bedroom on the right." He nodded in the direction of the other room.

Angie checked for herself.

"Do babies this age sleep through the night?" she asked.

"How would I know? Are you offering to take the two o'clock feeding?" He gave up trying to rein in the anger. Why didn't she do the smart thing and stay away from him? "What are you doing here, Angie?"

Something shifted in her expression, a subtle warning that he wasn't going to like her answer. She folded her hands in front of her. "There's been a development I didn't want to discuss over the phone."

"What development?" He was close enough to touch her, but he had no memory of crossing the room. He threw himself back into the chair he'd been sulking in before she'd arrived. "Is it Walker?"

"No. It's about the guy you shot at your house."

The compassion and regret in her eyes communicated the rest.

"Damn." He sank deeper into the chair, dust bunnies puffing from the cushions.

His first kill.

The first life he was totally responsible for removing from the earth.

"Damn," he said again.

There were no other words.

"It was self-defense." Angie crouched in front of him. Put her hands over his, which he realized were covering his face, and pulled them away. "You had no choice, Tony. It's not like you meant to kill him."

"Didn't I?" His fingers intertwined with hers, gripping hard enough to hurt, but she didn't pull back. "He was after Maggie. No one comes after my family. He was as good as dead when he stepped into my niece's room with a loaded gun."

"But Walker shot first."

"A technicality."

How could he feel so sick about taking out scum like Sam Walker's point guy?

"One mighty big technicality," Angie argued.

"Not big enough for our mayor." Laughter burned its way up his throat. "Henderson's going to love getting his hands on this."

Angie's earlier comment, the worry dragging her frown deeper, slammed into him.

"He's saying I took the guy out on purpose, isn't he?" Tony brushed away her hands.

"He's threatening an internal investigation," she confirmed. "I've told him I won't do it."

"Oh, really? You're going to tell my brother's boss to go to hell, and finish throwing away your career? What, now you're ready to choose me over the job you've built your life around?"

Say no. Please, say no.

Because he couldn't say it. Not anymore.

Lord, he needed her tonight. If she had any idea how much, she'd be running for the door.

"I won't target you with a useless investigation, just because the mayor's spoiling for a fight. Your brother won't let it happen, either. Even Oliver Wilmington's weighed in on your side tonight. You're not alone in this."

Why did she have to keep saying that? He was alone because that's how he chose to live. He didn't know how to *be* anything else.

He shoved away from both her and the chair. Away from the line he'd never been tempted to cross before. He faced off against her, his past and how much he wanted the mistake they were about to make.

But he couldn't look at her, only the floor.

"You're my superior officer. That means hands off, remember? Why are you doing this, Angie?"

"Because…" She swallowed, her whisper full of demons that were as ugly as his. Only he should have known she'd have the guts to face what he was still running from. "Because I care about you, Tony. Maybe more than is smart, but I can't seem to stop myself."

"You should go." He still couldn't look up.

"Tony…"

Angie reached for the words that couldn't possibly be enough.

She'd seen the heartbreaking loneliness in his eyes when she'd first gotten there. And that had settled it for her. Sure, she'd come to break the news about his shooter's death. But that didn't begin to explain why she couldn't walk away now.

"I'm not leaving," she said.

"You've delivered your message." His hands balled into fists. "I'll keep Maggie out of danger until you and Eric have Walker and his snitch in custody tomorrow. Now, go—"

"I'm not going anywhere. I'm not leaving you like this."

When he finally looked up, the desire and pain he no longer hid sucked her further in. He was breaking his enormous heart—the same one that would fight to the death to keep his brother's child safe—because the scared kid deep inside him, the one still running from nightmares, didn't know how to let anyone close enough to ease the hurt.

He cared about her. She was certain of it.

He might never be able to deal with how much, and that gave him the power to destroy her. But her instincts told her she belonged here with this man. And she was ready to follow the heart she hadn't listened to in three years. Ready to trust again, regardless of the risk.

"I'm not leaving you alone tonight." She grabbed hold of those fists and pried his fingers free until she could curl hers around them.

"I've got a teenager and a baby in the next room," he managed in a rough whisper. "I'm not alone."

The smile he forced would haunt her the rest of her life, she was sure of it.

"You're about the alonest person I've ever met, Tony Rivers." It was the ultimate gamble, but she took the initiative and brushed his lips with hers. And in that simple gesture, she gave him her heart. When his fingers clutched at hers, she squeezed back. "And I think that for the first time in a long time, alone isn't what you want to be."

"Since when did you become an expert on anything but getting through the day entirely on *your* own?" His words grazed her mouth, his kiss longer and deeper than her tentative one.

"Since I couldn't stop dreaming about being back at the bar with you, before things got so crazy." She hadn't wanted anything so badly in her life. "You're the part of my world that makes sense right now. The part that fits."

"Don't give me your heart, Angie." His eyes hardened with warning. "I don't know how to do anything but break it. Don't make this about forever, because I'm not the man who can give that to you."

"Then let's just make this about now." She inched closer, still not touching him except for their hands and lips. Trusting that he knew a whole lot more about love than he'd let himself believe. "Let's be a little careless, and see where that gets us."

Throwing his challenge from the other night back in his face earned her a fierce smile.

"You're a regular daredevil today, aren't you?" His big hand cradled her cheek.

"You seem to have that effect on me."

"I'm no good for you." His breath mingled with hers.

She drank him in.

"I guess I'll have to take my chances."

Her lips staked their claim. His opened so his tongue could feather over hers. He sat and urged her into his lap, where he caught her close with a groan.

"You don't take chances, remember?" he whispered.

"I do now, thanks to you."

His strong arms tightened around her. The smell, the taste, the warmth of him, were all the reward she'd ever need for breaking her rules.

Tony saw the woman inside her. She was a mess, just like her family thought. But to him that didn't mean she was broken. There'd been no room in her life for anyone. But here this man was, holding her in his arms, forcing her to feel what she'd never thought she'd feel again. Showing her that she hadn't been running after all. She'd been waiting, all these years, for the moment, the man, that would show her what it was to be alive again.

How could she have believed she could live without this?

"I… You…" He ducked his head away, even as his

hand found her breast beneath the uniform shirt it should be criminal to feel so feminine in. "I want you like I've never wanted anything in my life. But you deserve a man who can give you more than a night or two before he moves on. And I—" He kissed her as if he couldn't help himself. "I don't know how to be anything else. Not even for you."

"Then give me what you can," she heard herself say, when she should have been running for the door. He was all but promising to let her down, to be the player everyone in town thought he was.

But he was also the man who'd yanked her out of her shell and shown her what she was missing in life. What she was willing to risk everything to get back.

"Just be with me, Tony, please." She fished in her back pocket for the condom she'd been carrying around since their last night at the Eight Ball—when she'd promised herself this moment wasn't going to happen. "Let's not complicate this. I need you, and you need me. No strings. Just now. Tomorrow, we can both walk away if we want to."

She looked up into the eyes of the most eligible, most unattainable man in town, and she promised herself that if she saw pity, she'd walk right then and there. But what she found instead was the longing for closeness Tony was no longer hiding. At least, not from her.

He consumed her cry with another kiss.

I shouldn't be doing this, the careful voice inside warned.

But there was no stopping. Not this time. Even if it was only for one night, Tony Rivers healed what was broken inside her. And maybe, just maybe, she healed something inside him, too.

This time, neither one of them was walking away.

CHAPTER FOURTEEN

TONY HAD BEEN DYING SLOWLY for days, courtesy of the sexy, courageous woman falling to pieces beneath him.

But the best thing about dying, if you were very lucky, was finally holding heaven in your arms. And with each trembling, starving-to-get-closer kiss they shared, more of the cynical man he'd thought he was slipped away. The parts that feared anything that felt this good. This real.

They'd worked their way into the second of the tiny bedrooms. Had fallen onto Nina's fresh sheets. And in less than a minute, they were skin to skin, heart to heart. Protected by the condom Angie had opened with her teeth, but vulnerable in so many other ways. Tony had never understood people who talked about losing themselves in another person, but somehow it felt like Angie owned more of him tonight than he did.

He pushed back from where she lay. Let his gaze travel down her toned body. Lingered on every curve and valley. Then he took his time enjoying the slow climb back up. Every instinct screamed to bury himself inside her and bury the worry and second thoughts eating him alive—until it stopped being possible to think at all.

But he couldn't be that selfish. He wouldn't let himself.

"Is your arm okay?" She touched the bandage on his shoulder.

"I'm fine."

You're a bastard.

Let her go. Tell her to get the hell out of here.

"I'd be more worried about myself, if I were you." His hand cupped her softness, thumbed a nipple that pebbled at his touch. He'd played countless women, yet every second with Angie felt like his very first time. Like he wasn't playing at all. "You must be crazy."

"Yes—" The catch in her breath kicked his desire into overdrive. One of her hands went exploring, finding him aching to have her, throbbing as he fought for control. "I'm crazy for this. For you. You've been driving me cr—"

Her squeak was his reward when he lowered his head, his lips tasting what his hand had already treasured.

"You've been driving me crazy for months," she finished.

"Angie." He caressed where she'd grown moist and ready for him. Growled at the knowledge that she'd wanted this for as long as he had. "I don't… You should be with someone who can give you more. Someone who can—"

Damn it!

Love, *you idiot. Say the word.*

But he couldn't.

He shoved away until he was sitting beside her.

"You're not cutting and running on me, are you, Deputy Rivers?" She curled herself around him. Prey becoming huntress. Warmth and soft skin, and too much more, tempting him to caress.

"No, I'm giving you a chance to come to your senses, *Chief.*" He squeezed the curve of her hip. Palmed her bottom.

Perfection. The woman was the kind of perfection he'd never touched before. Freddie Peters was a damn fool!

"Well, don't do me any favors." Conviction rang in a voice gone sultry. No backing down, not from Angie. She arched into his touch. "Don't you dare try to protect me now—" Ran her hands up his chest. "Not now that I'm finally doing something careless like—" Pulled at his earlobe with her sharp, white teeth. "Like you always said I should. I'm a grown woman. A decade older than you, in fact. I know what I want."

And she wanted him. Needed him.

A woman who'd made a life out of not needing anyone.

She *was* crazy.

And he couldn't say no. Heaven help them both, he couldn't hold back a second longer.

"Darlin'," was all he managed to get out, then he covered her with his body and let go.

Magic. She was magic in his arms. A taste of something beyond him. Something fragile and rare, after years of nothing special. A promise of all he'd sworn he didn't need—the kind of complete devotion that could fill up the soul he'd let run on empty for too long. She was hot and sweet, with just enough roughness for him to know her desperation rivaled his own.

She was Angie. And for tonight, she was his.

Their lovemaking stretched on forever, until it was suddenly ending too soon. He sensed her fighting to hold on. But her pleasure was the final gift he had to have, after she'd given him so much already. Pinning her wrists over her head, taking away the control, he loved her. Worshipped her. Gave her back a speck of the perfection she'd already given him, simply by staying and sharing his lonely night.

When she tightened around him and began to fall, their eyes locked. Their bodies merged one last time. And with a groan, he joined her in a gripping spark of an ecstasy hotter than he'd ever known—already feeling himself pull away. Running, deep inside, from all she was offering.

Stop trying to handle everything alone.

But he couldn't. If it weren't for his niece and the baby sleeping in the other room, he'd already be working his way to the door. Smiling, laughing, but gone just the same.

Drawing her close as they shivered in the aftermath, kissing away the tears sprinkled across her cheeks, he clung to the sweetness of everything he had to let go of, before this went any further and he hurt her even more.

"DON'T GO. PLEASE, DON'T GO, too."

Tony was alone. The bad kind of alone—the kind when someone wasn't coming back.

Like when his mom hadn't come back, back before he could remember. But he did remember feeling alone the nights his dad had worked late, and no one had been home but his brother. He remembered dreaming about her sitting beside his bed, rubbing his back until he fell asleep. Stupid dreams.

But at least he still had his dad.

"See you after school, son," he remembered his dad saying that morning. *"Little League at six, right?"*

But no one had been home at five o'clock, when it was time to leave for the game. Or at six, when it was too late. No one had come to get him from the neighbor's house until his brother had.

Now Eric was angry and silent. Nothing new. But there were tears in his eyes. And that girl Carrinne had come with him.

And then the girl was saying something was wrong. His dad… There was something wrong with his dad.

Tony knew it was a dream, same as always. He could usually end the nightmare at will, but not this time. He tried to run, but he couldn't move. His heart raced. His lungs burned.

"There was a shooting," Carrinne was saying. *"At the gas station…. There was a guy…. Your dad was there with one of his deputies…. He saved another man's life…but, honey, your dad was shot…."*

Then suddenly, it was Angie with her arms around him, scaring him to death because she shouldn't be there, and she wouldn't let go.

Where was his dad? His dad couldn't be gone, too?

He looked wildly about for his brother—

"Eric?" he begged like a baby. He wasn't going to cry. Only babies cried. *"Where's Dad?"*

"Gone!" Eric shouted. *"He's gone, don't you get it? Just like Mom. Now they're both gone! We're totally alone!"*

"Eric, don't," Angie said—the Angie he knew should have been Carrinne, but dreams didn't work that way. Angie had slipped inside his desires, so here she was in his dreams, too. *"He's a little boy, and he's scared."*

"Daddy," Tony demanded. *"I want my daddy. I don't want to be alone. Where's my dad?"*

"He's gone...."

"No!"

Tony jackknifed to a seated sprawl, mostly back in the here and now. But a part of him was still drowning in the past.

"I don't want to be alone," the memories heckled.

The arms around his shoulders circled tighter, soothing the shuddering he couldn't stop.

"It's okay," Angie whispered—the real Angie now, even though the nightmare lingered, and in it she was still telling him that life as he knew it was over. That his dad, his family, was gone.

"God, Angie," he managed to say over the shock of remembering. "Make it stop."

It was a kid's reaction, but that's who he always became when he relived that night. A lonely kid who'd learned too young how to be strong, because he hadn't been given a choice to be anything else. He felt wetness on his face and wiped it away, hating the helplessness.

Why tonight?

Why did Angie of all people have to see him like this?

"I'm sorry." He gritted his teeth against the pain. "I...I can't make it stop."

"Don't try," she murmured, saying the right and the worst thing, all at the same time. Because with her permission, he lost what was left of his control and hauled her against him. "Let it out, Tony. I'm here. It's just me, and it's okay. You're not alone, darlin'. Let it go."

And he did. The fear and the loss. The pain burned in his chest as he clutched her closer and tried to breathe. Little-boy, it's-not-fair, why-is-it-happening-again pain. And all the while, she rocked him, rubbing his back. Promising him it was okay. It was a lie, but he let himself believe. Because she was there, and he finally wasn't alone.

Angie wanted to make it all right. And as he pulled her back into the covers still warm from their love, he almost let himself believe she could. Using her compassion shamelessly, he curled her closer and closed his eyes against the feel of her, even as the urge to run began to build anew.

MAGGIE STUMBLED OUT OF BED, the darkness broken only by the weak light shining through the half-closed door to the den. How long had her great-grandfather let her sleep?

Exhaustion and sadness and fear still making her brain fuzzy, she tiptoed away from the bed, leaving the thankfully still-sleeping baby to lie in his cradle of pillows. Max would need to eat as soon as he woke up, but the longer he slept the better.

Was her uncle back? Had they arrested Sam Walker while she was asleep? She still couldn't believe the man had come looking for her at the house.

Cringing at her baby-burped-on clothes, feeling gross and desperately in need of a toothbrush, she slipped through the door. Rubbing her eyes, she found her uncle sitting alone on the shabby old couch, watching the closed front door and looking so sad, her panic returned with a kick.

She'd never seen Tony anything close to sad before. He'd been plenty angry with her in the last twenty-four hours. Scared for her. But nothing like this. Not like something awful had happened he couldn't bring himself to face.

"What's wrong?" She sank to the edge of the lumpy chair beside him. The bandage on his shoulder brought tears to her eyes. "My mom and dad told me what happened. I'm so sorry Sam hurt you. Are you okay?"

At her touch, he blinked, looking away from the door as if he'd just realized she was there.

"Hey, kiddo. I'm fine." He gave her a wink that didn't quite work, and roused himself to run a hand through the hair spiking away from his head in a dozen different directions. "How'd ya sleep? Your great-grandfather headed home, but he'll be back later to wait for your folks with us."

Maggie stared at the way Tony wasn't quite looking at her. How there was no easy smile to go along with his fake hello.

"What's wrong? Why are you sitting out here looking like you've lost your best friend?"

Her uncle winced, then he stood.

"Everything's fine," he said. "I'm glad you got to talk with your folks. Angie's running interference down at the station. She's got everyone working overtime hauling Walker's goons in, thanks to the information you gave us. And with any luck, she'll have the Mortons here by the time Family Services knows anything about Max."

So where had her everything's-going-to-be-okay uncle gone? "What happened at the house? What aren't you telling me?"

Tony smoothed her bangs from her eyes. "Don't worry about it, honey."

"I know Sam and some other guy shot at you." She motioned to the bandage poking out from beneath a different T-shirt than the one he'd worn when he'd left. "How am I supposed to not worry about that? You could have been killed, just like Claire."

"But I wasn't." He knelt in front of her. "Your dad and Angie are going to take care of Sam, and that other guy won't be a threat to you or anyone else again."

"You mean he's... The other guy... He's dead?"

"Yeah, kiddo. I didn't have a choice."

"Oh my God!"

Her uncle had killed a man. Because of her.

Tony took her hand and squeezed. Something scary but strangely reassuring sparked in his eyes.

"Don't beat yourself up about any of this. He had a gun, and Sam fired first. I was defending myself, and more than that, they were there to stop you from talking about what you saw and heard at Claire's. I'd do the same thing again in a heartbeat. No way is Sam Walker getting anywhere near you. That's why you're still here. We have to keep you hidden, and no one in the department but me and your dad can know where you are. Not until we plug the leak that's funneling information to Walker."

Maggie forced herself to think, to keep it together. "You think there's a snitch in the department?"

"Walker has to have someone on the inside for him to have known to come after you. Someone we figure has been feeding him information for months."

"That's why you couldn't stop him before now?"

"Yeah." Her uncle's grip on her hands tightened. "That's why his guys are always a step ahead when we think we finally have a collar."

One of her dad's deputies, a snitch? But they were all so gung ho, busting it to beat back the drugs.

Her uncle was frowning. The same frown as before, different than his Sam Walker scowl. This was how he'd looked when she and her mom had left for their surgeries in New York, and he'd seemed afraid they wouldn't come back or something.

Angie had been with him, actually holding his hand as they waved goodbye at the airport. And she and Tony had been like best friends ever since. Maggie had always thought they were pretty cool together, the way they seemed to understand each other without even trying. And if anyone could give her uncle as good as she got, it was Angie—

Something Tony said stopped her. No one knew Maggie was there at the overseer's cottage but her family and…

"Angie was here, wasn't she?"

Tony stood, but he didn't answer.

"You said no one in the department could know I was here." But since when had Angie been just another deputy to her family? "Angie knows. She was here tonight, wasn't she?"

"Yeah." He turned away, but not before Maggie saw a flash of pain.

She checked out the window. The sun would be up in a few minutes.

"She was here all night?" she pressed, jumping to an unbelievable conclusion.

"Most of it." His shoulders sank. "The night's not over yet."

Angie had stayed all night when she wasn't supposed to be here. And Tony had been staring at the front door after she'd left, as if he could see straight through it to whatever he couldn't have on the other side.

Why are you sitting out here looking like you've lost your best friend?

Her uncle and his boss? Cool! It was about time. Except—

"You just let her go?"

Was he really that clueless? The guy had finally made time with someone besides the giggling groupies that followed him all over town, then he'd given Angie the kiss-off like all the rest!

Tony glanced back at her, rubbing at the whiskers covering his chin.

"Angie doesn't belong here, and she knows it."

"She's perfect for you." The idea was totally perfect. "You can't just give up. Our family doesn't give up, not when it's important. You told me to keep fighting for Claire. Isn't Angie important enough to fight for?"

His scowl grew.

"I'm checking on the baby." He headed for Max's bedroom. As if diaper duty was his number-one priority. "Your clean clothes are in the bag on the couch."

And then the man who hadn't blinked before putting himself between her and the scariest things she'd ever dealt with in her life slowly shuffled away.

CHAPTER FIFTEEN

"YOU LOOK LIKE HELL," Lissa said through the open window of her Mustang. She'd been waiting at the curb as Angie pulled into her driveway a little before dawn. "Where have you been?"

"Go away." Angie slammed her truck door behind her.

Her sister could read her like book, and Angie didn't have the stomach for it this morning. She needed a shower and a fresh uniform. And she needed to regroup before Eric arrived—hours before anyone but she and Tony were expecting. It was the twist in their plan they hoped would corner Sam and the leak.

"I have to be in the office for an early meeting." She'd already woken Martin Rhodes and Buddy Tyler and had told them to come in. "And I—"

"Didn't come home last night?" her sister finished for her.

"Lissa—"

"I *called*, Angie. All night. Mom and Dad heard

about the shooting at Tony's. It was all over the news. I tried to reach you at the station, but no one would put me through. I called here, and on your cell and over at Tony's, thinking you might be over there. I know how close you two have gotten. But he didn't answer, either—"

"We're colleagues, Lissa." Angie headed for her front door. "We're not *close.*"

Only a hint of what was raging inside her made its way into her voice. But she could barely push her key in the lock.

How could she have thought she'd survive this? Being careless and walking away unscathed clearly took more guts than she had.

"It's okay," she'd said to herself when she'd woken to the gray light of very early morning and the empty pillows beside her.

She'd found Tony sitting alone in the den. He hadn't looked up when she walked into the room. He hadn't seemed to know what to say, not that she'd needed to hear the words. The resignation clouding his face had said enough.

"It's okay. I understand," she'd assured him as she'd died a little more inside.

Easy come, easy go. No guarantees for the reckless and the careless.

Their chance for more than one night had been

slim at best, even before the nightmare had woken him. His complete vulnerability as he'd let her hold him had tipped their little experiment over the edge. She'd seen too many emotions he still couldn't share. Too much he still couldn't face.

So she'd calmly filled him in on her and Eric's conversation, and the plans for Walker's sting. She'd managed all business at its unemotional best. Right up until she'd dressed in her day-old clothes and retraced her steps to her truck. Once inside, she'd fallen apart.

"Tony and I are good friends," she said out loud, needing to hear the words herself.

"That's not what Karen Taylor told me. Her brother is friends with the bartender at the Eight Ball, and he said—"

Stepping inside her house, Angie did the unthinkable and slammed the door in her sister's face. Shoving the dead bolt home, she rested her forehead against the smooth oak door. She strongly considered cursing a blue streak. Only it wouldn't help. How could anything help after she'd gambled everything, again, and lost? Again.

Squealing tires announced Lissa's less-than-ladylike departure, leaving Angie alone.

It's okay.

How she hadn't choked on the words was a

mystery. And Tony had just sat there as she'd lied, the warmth and beauty of what they'd shared draining away until nothing remained but regret.

Tires squealed outside again. A door slammed. Then a fist pounded the door behind her.

"Ange?" Lissa—adorable right down to her signature French pedicure—sounded ready to try a few four-letter words herself. "I'm not going away, so I can stand out here in the front yard and scream at the top of my lungs about you and Tony, or—"

Angie swept the dead bolt back and yanked the door open. Grabbing her sister by the arm, she snapped, "Get in here!"

Lissa stumbled into the entryway of the cozy home Angie had worked up the down payment to finance only a year ago. Her sister squared off, ready for battle.

"Are you going to behave like a reasonable person?" Lissa demanded in the tone she used to discipline her kids.

"Not exactly." Angie headed for the kitchen and the coffee machine she prayed would fuel life back into her brain. An emotional hangover was out of the question today.

"Like you're *not exactly* seeing Tony Rivers? But you went on a date with him. And if I don't miss my guess, you just spent the night with the man."

Lissa tilted her head as she cataloged the wrinkles marring Angie's normally pressed-to-perfection uniform.

"Yesterday you told me to stop making my work my life." The can of coffee Angie pulled from the refrigerator landed with a thud on the counter. "Now you're pissed because I went on a date?"

The measuring spoon rattled against the tin as she scooped the dark brown promise of nirvana into her tiny coffeemaker. A coffeemaker perfect for one—or so the lady on the cable shopping station had promised one night when Angie hadn't been able to sleep.

More coffee landed on the counter than anywhere else.

"I didn't mean you should start dating the town's biggest hound dog. Tony's no good for you, Ange, and you know it." Her sister took over the spoon and the measuring, her expression gentling as she did. When the task was done, she faced Angie again, her anger spent. "He's going to drop you like he has everyone else, and I know what that will do to you."

Perfect for one.

Angie couldn't keep the phrase from rolling around in her sleep-deprived brain. She'd built her life to be perfect for one, and then Tony Rivers had blasted past every defense she'd erected. Straight through to a careless place inside that hadn't needed anybody but him. The place where she'd never be okay again, now that Tony was bailing.

You should go....

I'm poison....

"Angie?" Lissa asked. "Are you okay?"

"I'm fine!" She stumbled away and jerked the French doors open to her gated backyard. "I'm... I'm fine. I'm—"

Lissa wrapped her arms around her from behind. She rested her head on Angie's shoulder. "It's going to be okay."

"No. It's not." The childish half breaths between each word drove Angie to edge away—from both her sister and the backyard that promised fresh morning air and a safe place to cry. A complete meltdown and the explanation Lissa wanted were going to have to wait. "I have to get to the station."

She marched into the bedroom, scowling at her conspicuously un-slept-in bed.

"Are we back to that again?" Lissa demanded as she followed. "It's Sunday morning, your entire family's worried about you, and all you can think about is your career?"

"What career?" Angie dug around in the clean but unfolded laundry piled on the floor of her closet. "You must have seen the mayor on the news after yesterday's shootings. My shot at the election's over, and I'm too tired to even know if I care right now. All I have energy for is getting the last of the drugs out of this town. Oakwood's kids don't deserve to die, taking the stuff I'm supposed to be keeping out of their hands."

"Angie—" Her sister blocked her escape to the shower. "What's going on? What's wrong?"

"Nothing I can talk about." Her brittle smile hurt. But what didn't right now? "Everything's fine."

Lissa didn't stand in her way this time as Angie slipped into the bathroom. Her "I love you, little sister," worked its way through the closed door.

Angie perched on edge of the tub. Dropping her clothes to the floor, she let her sister's words wash over her like a healing brook in some kind of fantasy novel. Renewing, recharging, rebuilding her faith that she could get through this day. It wasn't her first trip to hell. She knew the score.

"I love you, too." Her reply echoed through the tiny bathroom.

She had no way of knowing if her sister even heard.

A moment later, the front door clicked closed as Lissa left. Finally, Angie was back in the comfortable world she'd created for herself. A world where she was safely alone.

A solitary haven where she no longer fit.

Good idea or bad, wise or not, she'd fallen in love

with Tony Rivers, and her life would never be the same again. Tony might not be able to return her feelings, but he'd given her a precious gift just the same. Her one careless night with him would forever be the moment when she'd realized she couldn't continue the charade she'd been living.

Being alone was still a lot safer than giving her heart to someone who might break it. But thanks to Tony, she'd finally accepted the truth.

For her, being safe just hurt too damn much.

"I DON'T HAVE TO IMPRESS upon you the importance of keeping this information between the three of us," Angie said to deputies Rhodes and Tyler less than an hour later, pointing to the printout on her desk. "The Rivers girl is on the run, and this new information means Eric's plane won't land in time for him to help talk her in. That leaves it to us to make sure she and that baby stay in Oakwood. She has information key to finding and stopping Sam Walker, not to mention pinning two murders on the bastard."

"Which two?" Buddy Tyler asked.

"I have ballistics back from yesterday. They confirm that the shot Walker fired at Tony matches the one that killed both Claire Morton and the other victim at Walker's apartment."

"So that clears Tony of both shootings," Buddy said.

His partner remained as silent as when the men had first arrived at her office.

"Yes." She couldn't stop the smile. The mayor's ammunition against Tony was now substantially depleted. Then she forced a grim expression. "But Tony's still not going to agree to bring Maggie in himself, not until we have Sam Walker under lock and key."

"You've talked with Rivers?" Martin asked, finally speaking up.

"No." Her disappointment played well with the scene she was trying to spin, so she let it fill her voice. "He's not taking my calls anymore. He made it clear yesterday he was keeping Maggie out of harm's way until the department did its job. He doesn't trust that anything he says to me won't be leaked again."

"So we're going to force his hand?"

"Something like that."

"That's got to be a bitch of a reversal, after—" Rhodes didn't finish his sentence.

"After?"

Buddy Tyler shifted his legs as tension spiked through the room.

Rhodes cleared his throat. "Well, it's not like it's a secret that the two of you—"

"Come on, man," Buddy warned. "This isn't the time—"

"No, it's not." Her clipped words shut them both up. "We need to move quickly. I called you two in because you've been on this case since the beginning. If we play our cards right, this should be a simple recovery job, and I don't have time to bring anyone else up to speed. I have to run interference with the mayor so everything's in place when Eric arrives. That means I can't be there to hold your hand. Don't think I've missed your opinion of my abilities, Deputy Rhodes." She nailed Martin with a furious glare. "But the safety of the sheriff's daughter is on the line, not to mention her testimony about yesterday morning. We need to bring Maggie Rivers in, without anyone knowing we have her painted. You think you can handle that?"

"The bus she's scheduled on leaves at twelve-fifteen?" Rhodes asked with a tight frown.

"Yes." Angie handed over the printout. "The seat's being held for an M. Rivers, bound for some out-of-the-way town in Virginia, where we know she was looking for the baby's grandparents."

"Doesn't sound like something Tony would do." Rhodes looked up from the paper. "He's got to know we'd be checking transportation in and out of town."

"I'm guessing Maggie's made plans on her own. The reservation's for only one person. Tony's determined to keep her out of danger. He wouldn't put her on a bus alone and send her somewhere he couldn't keep an eye on her."

"Which means she'll be out there unprotected," Buddy added. "If Sam gets to her first—"

"We're not going to let that happen." Angie folded her hands atop her desk. "With as little fanfare as possible, I need you two to bring in Maggie and that baby before Sam has a chance to track her down."

"And no one else knows about this?" Rhodes asked carefully.

"No." Angie pictured Tony playing it nice and easy, and gave her best impersonation. Unless she was dead-on convincing, this wouldn't work. "If I don't fill the mayor in this time, he's liable to trail us to the station and bust up the whole thing. But that's it. Once Eric lands and we have his daughter safe and sound, that'll be soon enough to release the details. Are the two of you on board?"

"Yes, ma'am." Buddy glanced at his ride partner expectantly.

"Sure." Rhodes shrugged in boredom. "What's the big deal, anyway? Two cops to bring in a nineteen-year-old girl."

Four cops, Angie corrected silently. There would actually be four cops at the station later that morning.

"Just keep your eyes open—"

"Who's in charge here?" an angry female screeched in the outer office.

Angie's door swung open.

"Where the hell is my grandbaby?" Betty Walker demanded, stepping in front of Rhodes and Tyler, her hair still caught up in the ratty curlers she'd slept in. "I've been calling this place since yesterday morning, and no one will give me a straight answer. My grandson's mother is dead, and you're hunting down my Sammy like he's public enemy number one. But can anyone tell me where a seven-month-old baby is—"

"Mrs. Walker." Angie stood. "If you'll have a seat, I'd be happy to explain where we are in the investigation. Give me a moment to finish with these officers."

"Go stuff your seat, lady. I want some answers!"

"Be ready to leave at nine-thirty." Angie dismissed her deputies with a nod, praying she'd planted enough information to hook their snitch. "Mrs. Walker, we're getting to the bottom of what happened yesterday," she said once she and Sam Walker's mother were alone.

"Get to the bottom of what, harassing my son? Your officers have *questioned* me half a dozen times, and my boy can't even come home. All because his girl was killed, when he had nothing to do with it. Don't think I don't know you're planning to ride your way into the sheriff's office by pinning a bunch of lies on my boy. So what if that trash he took up with goes off and does God knows what, and gets herself shot? What's that got to do with my son? Do you have any idea where my grandson is, lady?"

"Are you certain Max isn't with Sam?" Angie resumed sitting, outwardly unfazed by the other woman's tirade.

"Of course he's not with his father. Do you think I'd be here if he was?"

"So you have been in touch with your son, then?"

Silence smoldered through the room.

"Are you going to look for my grandbaby or not?"

Angie kept quiet and waited.

Betty's scowl deepened, along with the indignant flush darkening her ruddy complexion.

"That's all I get?" Betty fished in her jeans pocket and produced a pack of cigarettes. "I pay taxes, same as everyone else. But you ain't goin' to lift a finger to help a poor baby, whose—"

"Mrs. Walker, I can assure you that the safety of your grandson is as big a priority for this department as it is for your family. As is finding the person who killed his mother." The other woman's hand stalled in the process of putting a cigarette in her mouth. "You must all be devastated about Claire's death."

With a very ungrandmotherly sneer, Betty Walker stabbed a finger at Angie, complete with cigarette. "If it weren't for that little tramp, my son—"

"If it weren't for Claire Morton, there wouldn't be a baby for you to worry yourself over." Angie paused long enough for her statement to sink in. "I'm assuming you've been in touch with Claire's parents to let them know what's going on."

"I got no idea where that girl came from." Betty dug out a lighter, her cigarette wobbling between her lips with each word. "Besides, her parents have no place here. We're that baby's family, and I want to know what you're doing about finding him."

"There's no smoking in the station," Angie warned as her guest flicked the lighter.

Betty crushed both cigarette and lighter in her fist. "You ain't gonna tell me nothin', are you?"

Angie generated the best accommodating smile she could manage. "I'm not at liberty to discuss the details of any of our pending cases. But the department would appreciate any information you could supply about your son's whereabouts. Questioning him about yesterday morning's shootings might go a long way toward helping us find—"

"Like hell you just want to question him!" Betty braced her hands on the desk. "Your people have been crawling all over my place. Making all kinds of accusations about whatever you're finding in that shed I'd forgotten was even out there. You got no cause to say my boy has anything to do with anything you find in that place. He lives way across town."

"What makes you think we're looking Sam's way?"

"I hear things. I know you think he's behind all the shootings, the drugs. How dare you try to get me to testify against my own child! There are laws against that. I know my rights."

"Interesting that you would use the word *testify.*" Angie smiled away the woman's bluff. "Who said anything about charging your son, let alone putting him on trial? The department hasn't released a formal statement to either the paper or the TV news about yesterday's shootings. I'm afraid whoever you've talked with has given you some premature information."

"I ain't been talkin' with no one, lady." Betty Walker crammed her smokes back into her pocket. "I just know what I know."

Angie stood, her anger finally getting the best of her. A teenage girl was dead, and this woman couldn't care less. "Then know the sheriff's department is doing everything it can to bring to justice the people who contributed to your grandson losing his mother. And we're ending Oakwood's drug problems once and for all. I promise you, we won't stop this time, until Max and the rest of our citizens are safe."

Betty's vulgar suggestion of where Angie could shove her promises made it clear they understood each other. The woman's son was a prime suspect, and every second she spent flapping her yap at Angie only made the department's job easier.

"I'd watch my back, if I were you," Betty said as she turned to leave. "My son's got friends who don't take kindly to being harassed. Badge or no badge, I'd watch my step."

The door slammed in her wake. Angie resumed her seat and reached for the phone, more determined than ever to bury her useless angst over her one-night stand with Tony Rivers. She had a job to do, and she was going to kick its ass!

She dialed, picturing Sam Walker's face, and then Claire's and Maggie's, letting the fury flow through her and help her focus.

Time for step two in her and Eric's plan: notifying Mayor Henderson as late as possible of Maggie's supposed flight from Oakwood. They had to keep the man appeased, but also ensure he and the city council couldn't make trouble.

"This is Henderson," he groused. "I've been waiting for your call all morning, Officer. I'm getting ready to leave my house. You better have something good for me by the time I get to the station, or I'm going through with this afternoon's council meeting."

"That's why I'm calling, Mr. Mayor. I have an urgent development you need to be aware of."

TONY'S CELL PHONE RANG. The display read Dude.

"Eric." Tony walked to the other side of the room to talk, away from where Maggie and Nina were changing the baby's diaper—with Old Man Wilmington leaning over the women to supervise, of all things. "Where are you?"

Maggie looked up, but she didn't rush over to speak with her parents. With a newfound maturity, she watched and waited. It was like he'd witnessed his already wise-beyond-her-years niece grow up before his eyes.

"I'm about sixty miles outside of town." Eric's exhaustion after driving the entire night colored each word. "Carrinne should be making her connection in North Carolina right about now. She'll land as scheduled at the county airstrip, in case anyone thinks to check. She'll give Gordon's taxi service a call for a ride to the house."

"She knows to lie low until this is all over?" Tony asked.

"She promised me she would. It's the only way I'd agree to let her get on that plane."

Tony laughed at the thought of Eric trying to stop his wife from coming home to their daughter. "That and you needed a cover for being back three hours before scheduled."

"Where are things there?" his brother asked.

"Everything's fine. Angie briefed me, and she should be at the station by now setting things up—" Tony closed his eyes against the memory of her pale, solemn face. The pain she'd tried so hard to hide after she'd found him fighting off the dregs of his nightmare. After he'd shut down on her completely.

She'd filled him in on her and Eric's plan, then she'd left. She'd assured him she was okay. So, like a coward, he'd let her go—

"Tony?" his brother prodded.

"Oliver managed to get the mayor off Angie's back for a while," he said. "And we even have a few leads on Claire Morton's family. That leaves us sitting pretty until the showdown."

Eric listened past his brother's words. Tony's voice was too positive. Too fast. Too carefully upbeat, even for Tony. Too forced, in a way Eric had heard before, when the kid had been very young.

Chills raced down Eric's spine.

He struggled to focus on the road instead of the past. Shoved away his exhaustion. He had to keep moving. He had to get to Oakwood in time.

"What's going on with you?" he came right out and asked. Beating around the bush took too much energy.

"Nothing. We're all set," Tony assured him, and it might have been a good enough performance for anyone else.

Eric knew better. "You're spooked as hell. What do I need to know?"

"Nothing. Everything's in place. Sam's out on his ass, and he's got no place in town to run. He'll make his move today. All you and Angie have to do is be there to grab him when our Maggie shows up at the bus station. I've got both Nina and Oliver over here to keep Maggie company. Nina's even skipping her Sunday-school class this morning to help keep Mr. Max in fresh diapers. It couldn't get any better than that, right?"

Eric passed the slow-moving truck in front of him, then he hit the accelerator in the tiny car he'd nabbed at the airport rental place in New York.

"Look," he finally said. "If I don't get my mind back on driving, I'll end up a heap of junk on the side of the road. Spare me the runaround, and tell me what the hell's got you sounding like your world just got ripped out from under you."

The sigh that followed came with a mental image of Tony's head dropping.

"The guy with Sam Walker at the house yesterday, the one I shot? He died last night."

"Man." Eric still remembered his first kill. You always remembered. "You okay, kid?"

"Yeah. It was him or me, right?"

"Right."

Eric waited, his instincts telling him there was more.

"There's fallout from it?" he prompted.

"A little."

"Henderson?"

"We're handling it. Oliver's even covering my back until you get here. I'm on suspension, though."

"That's just departmental policy."

"Screw it, right?" Tony reasoned, far too reasonably.

Eric's thoughts exactly. And while they were at it, screw waiting patiently for the other shoe to drop.

"What's going on that you're not telling me, Tony? I've got enough on my hands without worrying about you, too."

"Then back off, will ya!"

"No problem, as soon as you tell me the rest."

"The rest is personal, and you—" Tony cursed. "Not now, okay."

Personal? His brother?

Damn.

"Tell me this isn't about you and Angie again." Like Eric really needed to ask.

"I—"

"Don't," he bit out. "You're right, this isn't the time, but you can bet your ass we're talking as soon Sam Walker's behind bars."

"There's no point—"

"There's plenty of point, man! If anybody knows that, it's me," Eric finished under his breath.

His little brother didn't lose his head like this over a woman. Over anything. He didn't play with fire the way Eric finally had, when he'd gambled on Carrinne and thankfully won a happy family as his grand prize.

"We're talking about this later, Tony," he said, knowing he'd pried all he was going to get out of his brother over the phone. He glanced at the dwindling gas gauge and began searching for an exit. "I've got to make a stop for some industrial-strength coffee and fuel, and I want to talk with Maggie for a minute. Is she up yet?"

"Yeah, sure." Tony's relieved, *"Maggie, it's your dad,"* came over the line.

"Dad?"

"How ya doin', darlin'?" Eric's eyes filled with tears at the sound of his daughter's voice. He blinked so he could see the road again. "You hanging in there?"

"Yeah. Everyone's taking good care of us. I wish you were back already. I'm so sorry I've caused everyone so much trouble."

"Sit tight and don't worry about a thing, honey. Your mother and I will be in Oakwood in a few hours, and we'll get to you as soon as we can," he promised the child who was a miracle he hadn't seen coming.

A miracle of warmth, and intelligence, and unconditional love. A future he hadn't deserved. Without Maggie and Carrinne, he'd still be a lost son of a bitch determined to go it alone and make the best of the empty hell he'd once thought was an okay life.

The hell that echoed through each of Tony's words now.

Eric was committed to giving his family every scrap of love and support they needed. Because they'd saved his sorry ass in every way a man could be saved. The way Eric was starting to believe his chief deputy and his brother might just be able to save each other.

What if Angie Carter, superior officer and all, was exactly what Tony needed to finally make his peace with the past?

CHAPTER SIXTEEN

AT TEN O'CLOCK ON THE DOT, Angie pulled her squad car over beside the deserted fruit stand on the outskirts of town. Eric's rental was already there.

"Tell me something good, Chief," he said as he stepped from the car and leaned back against the driver's door.

The man looked as rough as Angie felt, even though he was rumpled and wilted from his long drive, and her uniform was carefully starched and creased.

"Rhodes and Tyler are onboard," she reported. "They have no clue you and I will be tagging along. Henderson knows enough to keep him out of our hair while things play out, but I didn't tell him about the sting, or that you're arriving before Carrinne's plane lands. He thinks I'll be at the station, coordinating everything so I'm ready when you get in. And we've got a body double waiting in the wings—one of your sheriff friend's deputies from over in Pineview."

"I figured Dillon Reid wouldn't mind helping

out," Eric said, speaking of the neighboring county's sheriff whom he'd worked with several times in the past. "What about Tony?"

Angie couldn't speak for several seconds. Long enough for Eric's eyes to narrow.

"I spoke with him last night." Actually, it had been early this morning, a fact she had no intention of sharing with her boss.

"What did the two of you talk about?"

"The plans for the sting. That he needed to keep Maggie covered while we took care of the rest."

Dead silence followed.

"Are we sure Walker's going to show?" Eric finally asked. "It's a pretty stupid move, considering how much pressure you're putting on him and his people."

"He's desperate," she reasoned. "And desperate men make stupid decisions."

More silence.

"I guess desperate women do, too, huh?"

He knew. Angie's stomach sank to her knees. He knew about her and Tony.

She swallowed. "I don't know what you think—"

"I think I haven't slept much in forty-eight hours, and neither have you." He folded his arms in front of himself, crossed his legs at the ankles. "And I think I could kill Sam Walker with my bare hands for putting my family through this. He'd better show this morning, or I'm going to hunt him down and shoot him like a dog."

"He'll show. Guys like Sam don't know how to quit when they're ahead."

Eric nodded, shifting his feet and studying the cracked red clay beneath them. "And I think that if you and Tony are right for each other, then by all means, risk whatever you can afford to gamble, Angie. But before you put your job on the line, you need to understand my brother's aversion to latching on to things he might lose."

She laughed. It was either that or scream.

"Oh, trust me. I understand."

Eric's frown softened. "You're setting yourself up for a pretty big fall. After everything that happened with you and Freddie, I know damn well you're not an easy-come, easy-go kind of woman. Why are you doing this?"

Her heart felt as if it were trying to run right out of her chest.

"Because, I—" She choked on the answer she hadn't been completely honest about when she'd given it to Tony.

I care about you, Tony.

Yeah. *Caring* was all that ached inside her.

She checked her watch. "We should get going."

"Yeah," Eric said, scratching the hair at his temple.

"Tony didn't really want to talk about it either. It's pretty damn lucky for you both that we don't have the time to get into it."

POSITIONED TO THE RIGHT of the bus station's main entrance, Angie craned her head to see Eric on the other side of the building. They were hidden from Rhodes's and Tyler's view, but from their vantage they'd be ready to intervene as soon as trouble started.

"Dispatch, let the chief know we've got our girl," Buddy Tyler reported over his radio, using the code they'd agreed on until Maggie Rivers was in hand. Angie, only twenty feet away, heard each word through her hands-free earpiece.

Tyler and Rhodes were on foot and in plain clothes, closer to the front of the building, watching along with Eric and Angie as a lone figure worked her way up the steps to the bus station doors. The young woman only she and Eric knew was a stand-in kept her head down and the blanket-swaddled bundle in her arms clutched protectively close. A sweatshirt, complete with a concealing hood, completed her costume. She was stick-thin like Maggie, and just as tall. To anyone glancing her way, she'd easily pass for a teenager working hard not to be noticed.

She disappeared inside the building—after which the Pineview deputy had been instructed to ditch the rolled-up towel she'd been holding like an infant and scan the area for complications.

Angie's hand hovered over her holster. She forced the level, calm breaths that kept her heart rate from affecting her reflexes.

"Repeat," Tyler said. "Let the chief know we're a go."

But before the deputies could move from the bench they'd been hanging next to, a figure dressed in jeans and a Redneck by the Grace of God T-shirt, oversize bill cap and sneakers approached the steps at a saunter. A suspicious bulge behind his belt buckle screamed trouble.

It could have been any number of the kids that hung out downtown on slow Sunday mornings. Except there was no chance this wasn't Walker, tipped off by one of her deputies to an easy score. No way would he leave silencing Maggie once and for all to someone else.

Angie's fingers itched to ring Martin Rhodes's neck.

"Dispatch, we may have a problem," Tyler announced. "Stand by."

He and Rhodes fell in step behind Walker as the man approached the middle of the steps.

"Don't move," one of the deputies called out.

Stunned, Angie realized it was Rhodes who'd spoken.

The figure in the sweatshirt pulled the weapon

from his jeans and rounded on the two deputies. Rhodes and Tyler were ready for him, their guns trained in a textbook standoff.

Angie rounded the corner of the building, approaching the scene from the men's right side. Rhodes glanced her way briefly when he sensed her approach, but to his credit the man's attention instantly returned to their suspect.

A suspect who most definitely wasn't Sam Walker.

"Holy hell," Angie exclaimed, her own gun aimed at Garret Henderson.

"Drop it," Martin commanded the mayor's teenage son. "Damn, boy, don't mess with us about this. What are you doing here? Drop the gun."

Garret Henderson, the mayor's eighteen-year-old pride and joy, stood as if hypnotized, staring through strung-out eyes at the three armed deputies before him, wielding a shaking automatic pistol.

"He— He said this would be a no-brainer," the teen blurted out.

"Who said, son?" Eric, his own weapon trained on the kid, stepped into view on the boy's left. He approached as slowly as Angie.

"What the hell are you two doing here, Sheriff?" Rhodes demanded.

"Keep your mind on the mark, Deputy," Eric bit out. "The chief and I will explain everything later."

As if they'd choreographed it, each officer carried out his role in the regulation dance that should get them all out of the standoff in one piece. It was thankfully still early. There was no one else around to add fuel to the already volatile exchange.

"He… I told him she'd be alone," Garret mumbled. "Without her stupid uncle. He said there might be one cop here, maybe two, but that was all. Everyone else was hunting him down. She'd be easy to get away from the deputies…. But to bring a g-gun, just in case. Just in case!" Garret's pistol jerked toward Eric, then Angie, then returned to point at the two deputies directly in front of him. His glassy eyes widened and filled with tears. "In and out… Just d-do it, then run. Then he'd give me more stuff…. And my old man wouldn't have to know…."

"Do what, kill my daughter?" Eric inched closer. "How did you even know Maggie would be here?"

"Stay back!" The kid made another pass, pointing the gun at each one of them. He was in bad shape, if he believed he could hold them back for long. "I hear things at the station. And from my dad, when he's dragging me around everywhere. Things everyone thinks I'm too st-stupid to understand. Didn't take much to f-figure this out. To get in good with S-Sam again. My information's always top rate." Garret laughed. It was an ugly, bottomless sound. "You're not supposed to be here, Sheriff…. Quick and easy, he said. Our secrets would be safe, and I'd be back in time for my ma's Sunday dinner."

"Look at me, son." Rhodes moved a step closer, his voice soothing and nonthreatening. A cop's secret weapon when talking down a perp who didn't want to hurt anyone, but was out of control enough to be capable of almost anything. All of this from a man Angie had been certain was dirty. "You're already caught. There's nowhere to run. You've been feeding information to Sam Walker for months, haven't you? And he's been stringing you along with drugs. Then he threatened to tell your old man, right? Before you knew it, you were in too deep to get out and you couldn't say no."

"You— You don't know anything. You don't have jack on me." Garret began feeling his way backward up the steps. "Do you know who my father is, asshole? You can't make anything stick. Not to me."

Each of them followed, one step at a time. Maggie's double slipped soundlessly through the station's front door and waited as Garret backed toward her.

"Your daddy's not going to bail you out of this one, Garret," Eric said. "So don't do anything you're going to regret. Put the gun down, and lift your hands over your head. You don't want to hurt anyone."

"I already have, don't you get it! The shit that killed Travis and that New Year's kid. They got it from me. It was Sam's stuff, but I sold it to them."

"So you've made some mistakes." Eric inched another step closer, his voice perfectly calm. Perfectly reasonable. "Don't make things worse by—"

"Go to hell, man." The kid's gun locked onto Eric's chest. The muscles in his arm tensed to fire.

"Drop it. Now!" Rhodes had the best position. He made his move.

Garret rounded on him. They struggled and the kid's gun fired before Rhodes could grab it.

Buddy Tyler crumpled to the steps, then Garret swung his shooting arm wide. The barrel of his gun bashed into Rhodes's temple, sending Martin to his knees, stunned by the blow; his own weapon skidded away. The freaked-out craziness in Garret's eyes said he was ready to empty every bullet into the deputy's back.

Angie, the Pineview deputy and Eric swarmed.

Angie got there first.

She deflected Garret's weapon as the Pineview deputy moved in. Eric kicked the kid's feet out from under him, and Angie took him down. Garret landed in a sprawl.

"Get off me," the kid growled, stronger than he should have been, courtesy of the narcotics surging through his veins.

She forced him onto his stomach. Twisted his arms behind his back and added a knee to the center of his spine for good measure—neutralizing the kid while Eric ripped the gun away. Martin Rhodes surged to his feet and wiped at the blood trickling from the gash at his temple.

"Turn me loose, bitch!" one of Oakwood's former choirboys snarled.

"Shut your mouth." Rhodes yanked the kid's head up by his hair while Angie clipped cuffs around Garret's wrists. "You make me sick, coming after a defenseless girl and a baby, just to score another hit."

He helped Angie drag the teenager to his feet. The deputy's smirk was one of grudging respect.

"That was the best tackle I've seen yet, Chief." For the first time, her title didn't sound like a put-down coming out of the man's mouth. "Thanks for the backup."

She nodded in acceptance. Dealing with her misjudgment of Martin Rhodes would have to wait until later. Much later. Together, they cast worried glances to where Eric was checking on Buddy.

"Dispatch," Rhodes said into his com link. "We

have an officer down at the bus station. We need an ambulance immediately. Repeat, officer down at the bus station."

"It's only a flesh wound, man," Eric reassured the younger officer.

But the gaze he lifted to Angie wasn't nearly as calm as his voice. Something was wrong.

Why had Sam sent a kid to grab Maggie, when it was so crucial that the only eyewitness to yesterday morning's homicides be silenced? Garret's information, that Angie had sent only two deputies, one of them a junior officer, to deal with things at the bus station, should have been the perfect opening for Sam to take care of business. Unless he'd guessed there was more going on and had sent Garret to take the fall.

Which meant he hadn't expected Maggie to be at the station at all. And he'd guessed she was somewhere else entirely.

Eric hauled Garret away from Angie and Martin.

"Where's Sam Walker?" he demanded, shaking the kid by his shirt.

Garret should have been terrified. Lord knows, anyone in his right mind would have been at the sight of Oakwood's sheriff looming over him in a rage. But the kid laughed up at Eric, his eyes unfocused, his head lolling back and forth as he babbled.

"Get the girl," Garret crooned. "He said, whatever

it takes, today's the day we're getting the girl and shutting her up for good…. Sam said to get the girl…get the girl…."

"I CAN'T BELIEVE YOU'RE HERE," Maggie cried, throwing herself into her mother's hug.

"Neither can I," her great-grandfather grumped, frowning right along with her uncle. "Carrinne, if someone saw you come over here—"

"No one saw me." Her mom wiped at Maggie's tears, and then her own. "I had Gordon drop me and my luggage at the house, then I took the back way over. I was careful."

"Eric wanted you at home until we have Sam in custody," Tony chimed in.

"I couldn't stay away." Her mom sniffed as Nina bustled closer and made it a group hug. "Everyone who matters thinks Maggie's on her way to the bus station right now. No one's looking for her here."

"You took an enormous chance, Carrinne," Maggie's great-grandfather said.

"Well, I'm here now. Are you saying you want me to leave?" Her mom stiffened and turned to stare at the men. "Since when do the two of you agree on anything, anyway?"

She had a point.

It was still a shock to Maggie, seeing her uncle and

great-grandfather as a unified front. But the whole morning had been that way. As if they were some close, kinda freaky nuclear family.

Her mom turned back, her smile a little shaky but as strong as always. "You're one lucky lady, to have all these people pulling together to help you."

Maggie could only nod. It was like she'd gotten to know her uncle all over again, only this time she'd met the real Tony. He'd risked everything for her. He'd killed a man to protect her. And for the first time, she was starting to believe her great-grandfather really cared about her and her mom. And Nina had been there, too.

All of them had saved her from the horrible mess she'd made out of trying to help her friend.

"I screwed up so bad with Claire, Mom." Everything rushed back. Everything she'd worked so hard not to think about all morning. "I should have helped her sooner. None of this would have happened. If I'd only—"

"Shh." Her mom's hug felt even better the second time. "You did everything you could. You've been so brave, honey. I couldn't be any prouder of you."

"Uncle Tony's been brave," Maggie rushed to say, catching Tony's wink over her mom's shoulder. "He and Angie were so mad at first."

"I don't think *mad*'s the right word," Tony corrected over Max's whimpers from where Nina now cuddled the baby near the couch. "You scared the hell out of me, showing up with blood all over you—"

"Okay, no blood talk." Her mom's hands skimmed down Maggie's arms as if searching for boo-boos, like she had when Maggie was a little girl. "We just got you healthy again, sweetie. I can't stand the thought of you coming so close to danger again."

Maggie tried to stop the shaking, fought to be brave like everyone said she was. But the shock of seeing her mom, plus the reality of everything that had happened, was suddenly too much. She hurled herself back into her mother's arms. Then her uncle Tony's hand was on her shoulder. Looking behind him, she glimpsed her great-grandfather's concerned frown.

"I've been so scared." She couldn't stop the shaking. The tears. "I tried not to be, but I can't stop seeing Claire after Sam shot her…and I couldn't do anything to help her…."

"It's okay to be scared, honey." Her mom smoothed a hand down Maggie's hair. "You've held it together for Claire and Max. You did everything you could on your own. Your family's here now to help. You don't have to be brave anymore."

"Just let it go, kiddo. You're not alone," Tony's deep voice promised, full of almost fatherly understanding.

Then she felt him tense, a second before she heard footsteps on the front porch. The door crashed open, knocking her great-grandfather to the ground.

"Anybody moves, and I start shooting," an angry voice shouted.

Maggie and her mom were jerked behind her uncle's broad back, but not before she caught a terrifying glimpse of the man pointing a gun at them.

"Now what do we have here?" Sam Walker smiled at the room full of the people Maggie loved.

His grin widened as he stared down the barrel of the automatic handgun her uncle pulled from the waist of his jeans—a twin of the one in Sam's hand.

"Look's like I'm a little late for the family reunion," Max's father said. "And what a surprise to see you here, Maggie, what with all the helpful information your uncle and our Chief Carter planted about you skipping town on a bus. But then I started thinking maybe that wasn't such a good lead after all. I've been hearing rumors there was some odd stuff going on over here in the high-rent district. Like the maid missing Sunday school. Your mom being back in town, but one of my guys seeing her walking away from your house about an hour ago. He lost her somewhere over on Crabapple, but it didn't take much to slip down here and check things out. And lookie at what I've found. No one home at the big house, but there's a party going on in this moldy old place. Bring that kid over with the rest of them, lady," he said to Nina, who was still holding Max.

"Don't be stupid, Walker." Tony motioned for Nina to stay put. "Drop the gun."

"Now why would I do that?" Sam's sneer looked more desperate than intimidating.

Something told Maggie desperate was worse.

"Because you may be a coward and a bully, but dying isn't your style. Where are your legions? You never travel alone. They're running for the hills, aren't they, the ones who aren't in jail? Dumping you like a bad habit. You can't kill everyone here, not by yourself. And you won't get me before I do some fairly painful damage to that body you're always so proud of pumping up at the gym."

"Maybe I'll take you out first," Sam threatened.

"What about Max?" Maggie poked her head around her uncle, despite Tony's best efforts to keep her completely hidden. She was ready to take Sam out herself. "He's your baby. If you start shooting, he'll get hurt like Claire was. What's wrong with you?"

"To hell with the baby!" Sam emphasized each word with a wave of the gun. "I'm here for you, sweetheart. You and that mouth of yours have pissed me off for the last time. You've ruined everything!"

"Be still, honey." Her mom placed a hand on Maggie's arm.

"You'll have to get through me first, Walker." Tony was dead serious, ready to die, ready to kill. Whatever it took to keep the people he cared about safe.

"Really?" Sam glanced to where Maggie's great-grandfather was struggling to sit up. He pressed the muzzle of his gun to the man's temple. "Maybe I'll start with this old coot instead, and see where that gets me."

"No!" Maggie launched herself away from her mom and uncle and toward the man who'd killed her best friend. "Leave my family alone!"

"No problem." Sam grabbed her by the throat and hauled her against him. He kicked her great-grandfather in the chest, sending him crumpling back to the floor.

"No!"

Sam's hand choked off her squeal. Using her as a shield, raising his gun to her head, he edged toward the door.

"Maggie!" Her mom was a fighting fury trying to escape Tony.

Her uncle somehow managed to hold her back and still keep his gun trained on Sam.

"Lord have mercy," Nina exclaimed over Max's wails.

"Don't move another inch, Walker!" Tony snarled.

"Or what?" Sam wanted to know.

He skidded to a stop at the sound of approaching sirens. His grip tightened on Maggie's throat, but she could feel the trembling in his arm and fingers. His filthy hair brushed her cheek as he looked from one terrified grown-up to another.

Then came a chuckle worse than any curse word she'd heard in her life.

"Looks like we have ourselves one hell of a cliff-hanger," Sam said.

Tires squealed up her great-grandfather's drive-way. Footsteps pounded through the woods outside.

"Drop it, Walker," her dad shouted from close by.

"It's going to be okay, kiddo," Tony promised, his eyes never glancing away from Sam.

He'd said that to her before, just yesterday. And he'd been right. She'd made it through what she'd thought would be the worst day of her life, because he'd been there to help her.

As Sam cursed and dragged her back into the house and out of the open doorway, Maggie began to pray that she could trust her uncle's promise one last time.

CHAPTER SEVENTEEN

"HOW DID I NOT SEE this coming?" Angie asked as she and Eric crouched behind an enormous oak tree.

More and more backup pulled into the Wilmington yard by the second, sirens and lights blaring like the midway at a demented carnival. Angie had told them to make their approach as loud and intimidating as possible. So far the tactic had stalled Walker while she and Eric worked on plan B.

"We were waiting for our man across town. Tony was covering things here," Eric bit out, hell raging in his eyes as he clung to his trademark calm. "You handled everything by the book."

"Screw the book." Panic owned her. She'd never felt so paralyzed as when they'd arrived to find Maggie clutched in Sam Walker's arms with a gun pointed at her temple. "I let this get personal. I should have hauled Maggie's butt into the station yesterday. Thrown Tony in jail, whatever it took to protect them."

"And when Walker's family took Max and disappeared, what then?" Eric snapped. "Or when my daughter ran and put herself in even more danger by being out in the open?"

"I—"

"You followed your gut, Chief!" His half-crazed stare called her to the mat. "You were creative, used your head, and you and Tony took the chances you needed to. You got us this far without losing another innocent life. Garret was a wild card. Sam outsmarted us this time. Get over it, and get your head out of your ass. Help me get Maggie and Tony out of that shack in one piece!"

"I want to talk with this girl's daddy!" Walker shouted from where he'd dragged Maggie back inside. "I wanna talk with the sheriff, and I mean now, man!"

Angie swallowed Eric's command, then scanned the half-dozen officers in position between them and the cottage. Her deputies were hiding behind trees or shrubs, poised for action. Waiting for orders. And Tony was inside, his sole focus on keeping Maggie safe.

Eric was right, the odds were in their favor. Sam Walker was going down.

"You better get off your butt and talk to me, Rivers," Sam shouted. "I've got your lady *and* your little girl, and they brought along lots of friends for me to choose from when I start shooting."

"Carrinne!" Eric would have sprinted around the

tree if Angie hadn't grabbed his arm and dug in as he cursed and struggled to pull loose.

"Stay down!" she barked. With her other hand, she thumbed her communicator. "Baker, who has a visual on the inside of the house? We need a head count."

"Let me go, Angie! He's got my wife in there, too." Eric snarled. "Maggie and Carrinne... Tony can't protect them both."

"Not on your life, Sheriff. You either pull yourself together, or I'll have one of the boys lock you in the back of a squad car. Let's take it slow, let's be sure, and let's nail this bastard."

She gave Eric an instant replay of his get-it-together glare, even as she fought instincts that screamed for her to storm the tiny house right along with him. Tony, a man who'd rather die than watch another part of his family be taken away, was facing down a maniac who didn't care which Rivers he killed first.

Don't do anything stupid, Tony. Give us a chance to help you.

"We have one shooter, five civilians, and it looks like a baby," Baker responded. "Walker has the Rivers girl just inside the door."

"Okay, Eric," she said, turning him loose and slugging his shoulder. "Think! You and Carrinne used to sneak around this place. Tell me what you know about that house, and how I can get inside without Walker seeing me."

Because she was the one going in there and finishing this. The Rivers family had been through enough. Tony had been through enough. It didn't matter that the man couldn't let himself care for her the way she needed. He'd given her back her life by helping her see that she'd buried the best part of herself for years. He'd helped her see she was all woman inside, and she always had been. Forget Freddie's disappointment when she hadn't turned out to be what he wanted. She deserved better than him, and she always had.

She could finally risk loving again, no matter the hell she'd pay if it didn't work out. All because her best friend's love, if only for one night, had reminded her how to love herself.

Tony, Eric and their family had risked and won the greatest battle she'd ever seen, simply by finding each other and making their lives together work. She'd be a lucky woman if she found a speck of something that perfect for herself. And when this was all over, she was damn well going to start looking.

"ERIC KNOWS ABOUT the back door off the kitchen," Carrinne whispered softly to Tony. So softly, Walker couldn't hear on the other side of the room where he still held Maggie. The guy was staring into the heavily wooded yard.

"It's locked," Nina chimed in, while Tony fought to sort through the possible next steps.

He wasn't losing his niece or his sister-in-law this way.

"There's a key on top of the doorjamb," Carrinne whispered in response.

"Put your gun down, man!" Walker demanded as he spun back in their direction, Maggie wheeling around with him. "I swear I'll drop her if you don't."

Tony hesitated, knowing the drug dealer was desperate enough to do just about anything. But giving up his weapon would shift power dangerously in Walker's favor.

"Do it!" Walker pulled Maggie's head back, using her hair, until she whimpered. He jabbed his gun under her chin. "I got nothin' to lose." He shifted to yell back out into the yard. "Get me the stinkin' sheriff. I wanna deal, if he wants his girl back alive."

Carrinne's hand squeezed Tony's elbow, a string of very un-Carrinne-like sobs covering the sound of footsteps crunching around their side of the house. The side leading to the kitchen door Walker wouldn't know anything about.

Eric would be inside any second.

"I'm putting it down," Tony announced. He lifted his arms in the air, slowly uncurling his fingers from his automatic, making it clear he was no threat. "No worries, okay man? Just be cool."

"This is Sheriff Rivers," his brother said over a loud speaker. "You're surrounded, Walker. We have Garret Henderson in custody. Once he's detoxed, he'll be filling my deputies in on the details of your organization. We've got half your men in jail already. It's over."

"It's not over until I say it's over!" Walker's gun locked onto Tony as he yelled back to Eric. "Everybody'd better back the hell away and do what I say."

Tony bent at the waist, slowly going through the motions of giving up his weapon. Counting off seconds. If Eric was out front talking, his brother would trust only one other person to be sneaking through the back door to catch Walker off guard.

Damn it!

"What's it going to take to end this?" Eric's continuing dialogue covered the *snick* of the back door's lock. "Tell me how to get my family back."

"Maggie here stays with me," Walker announced as Tony laid the gun firmly on the coffee table, his hand hovering over it as he let go. "I want a car out of here, and no interference when I leave. Not if you

ever want to see sweet Maggie here again. You—"
He waved his gun for Tony to rejoin the others. "Step
away from that table. I won't miss this time like I did
back at your house."

Out of time, left with nothing to do but wait for
someone else to make a move, Tony caught sight of
Oliver Wilmington stirring and opening his eyes. The
man found and held Tony's stare. He curled his fists
around his cane and waited for Tony's signal. God
love the old curmudgeon.

Tony's hand still hovered over his gun. He
stared down the dead man who'd dared threaten his
family again.

"Last chance, Sammy," he said. "Are you really
ready to die today?"

"Move away from the gun," Walker threatened.

"Uncle Tony," Maggie squeaked.

A faint rustle in the kitchen behind him caused
Tony to smile reassuringly into his niece's terrified
eyes. Angie was inside, he was certain, covering his
back as she said she always would.

Always. A word he was only now starting to let
himself believe in.

"It's going to be okay, kiddo." He winked.

Then he relaxed his entire body so he could move
freely, whatever that next move would be.

"Freeze, sheriff's department!" Angie burst into

the room, gun raised, giving Tony enough time to retrieve his own weapon.

"Turn the girl loose," he growled.

"Go to hell! Ahh—" Walker yelped as Wilmington's cane made bone-splintering contact with the man's knee.

Walker went down hard, cursing and dragging Maggie with him. Nina dropped to the ground behind the couch, shielding herself and Max from danger. Carrinne lurched forward to grab Maggie, distracting Tony the second it took to drag Carrinne back behind him.

One lousy second. But before he could refocus—

"Drop it, asshole!"

Walker had lost hold of Maggie, who'd crawled to her great-grandfather's side, the harsh sound of the man's breathing making her whimper. But Walker's gun had found a new target.

Dead center at Tony's chest.

Tony's weapon hung useless at his hip.

"Down!" Angie shoved him and Carrinne aside. She fired an instant before Sam Walker did.

Tony broke Carrinne's fall, then rolled her beneath him. A sickening gasp above them was followed by the thud of Angie falling in a soft heap.

"Bitch!" Walker looked up from the blood spreading down the front of his shirt. "Stupid bitch!"

He raised his gun with a wildly shaking hand.

"No!" Maggie grabbed his arm, yanking it and the gun upward.

Walker pulled free, his gun now trained on Tony's niece.

"Say hi to Claire for me," the man snarled, a split second before Tony fired and blew the left side of his head off.

"Maggie!" Carrinne screamed, scrambling from beneath Tony as deputies flooded the house, Eric leading the charge.

"Angie!" Tony bellowed, leaving his brother to care for their family. He turned her onto her side, pressing his hand to the belly wound near her waist that was seeping blood. "Darlin', look at me. You're okay, you hear me? Hold on. Just hold on!"

He was drowning in her cat-green eyes. She started to smile, then she groaned, squeezing her eyes shut with a gasp of pain.

"Tony?" she whispered so softly he had to bend closer to hear. "Did I… Maggie?"

"You got Walker," he crooned. "Maggie's fine. Everyone's fine."

His heart wouldn't beat. His lungs wouldn't work. Angie had to be fine.

"Someone get over here and help her!"

"The paramedics are on their way." Eric gripped

his shoulder. "Everyone else is okay, except Oliver looks like he has a few broken ribs. How is she?"

Tony couldn't speak. He'd never been so terrified in his life.

"I'll wait for the ambulance outside." Eric squeezed his shoulder once more before leaving.

"Don't go...." Tony swallowed against the words he whispered into Angie's ear. The same words he'd cried last night in her arms, when he'd woken from a nightmare to the safe feeling of her body wrapped around him. Only this time, she was bleeding to death in his lap. "Don't you dare do this, Angie Carter. You hear me? Why the hell did you do this? Don't you quit on me now."

He was babbling, but he couldn't stop.

She was leaving. She'd made him care about her, damn it. She'd promised she'd have his back. She couldn't leave. He wouldn't let her.

"Darlin', please stay with me." With the hand not applying pressure to her wound, he smoothed baby-soft hair from her eyes. "Why did you do it, Angie? Why didn't you take Walker out, the hell with him shooting me first?"

"'Cause," she said even more softly than the last time. She gave him the same sad smile as when she'd walked away from his silence that morning. "L-love you."

And when her eyes closed this time, Tony felt the frozen heart of the lonely little boy inside him shatter into a million pieces.

"UNCLE TONY?" MAGGIE said tentatively from the open door of the hospital waiting room. Brave, sweet Maggie.

Tony couldn't look up. He couldn't think. Angie had been in surgery for hours.

L-love you.

From the start, Angie had been the one who'd said they couldn't be together. As usual, she'd been right. Their friendship had seemed so safe at first, because like him she hadn't had the guts to want anything more. But over and over again, she'd put herself on the line for him. She'd been willing to risk everything, to help him, to have him. Her career, her life.

Because she…

She couldn't be in love with him. He wasn't the kind of guy women loved. He'd made sure of it by always being the first to walk away.

Except this morning, he'd been the one left behind when Angie walked. He'd been the one wishing she'd find a way to want more, and then show him how to believe, too.

And she had.

L-love you.

"Tony?" Maggie sat next to him, baby Max snuggled in her arms, sucking hard on a bottle.

She'd changed into hospital scrubs, probably at the same time she'd showered off the splatters of Sam Walker's blood that had covered her. Tony had no idea how she'd gotten to the hospital. With her mom, probably, or in the ambulance with her great-grandfather. The EMTs would have checked Maggie and the baby out by now. And he'd heard the Mortons had finally returned Angie's messages. That they were on their way in from Texas.

Eric would still be at the Wilmington place, dealing with the scene and the press. The mayor had shown up as Tony left in the ambulance with Angie, demanding an accounting of the morning's events. Then he'd stared in devastated silence as his son's involvement in Sam Walker's activities had been revealed.

"Everything's going to be okay." Maggie grabbed his hand. He'd once promised her the exact same thing. "You'll see."

Tony glanced across the crowded waiting room at Angie's frightened parents. Her three sisters and their husbands, and their two point five kids apiece. All of them terrified. Waiting to see if Angie had gotten herself killed for a man who didn't know how to be what she deserved.

They'd stared his way from time to time, particularly Angie's closest sister, Melissa. No doubt wondering what he was doing there, when the rest of the off-duty deputies were waiting in the hallway. Including Buddy Tyler, who'd been on his feet again as soon as an E.R. nurse had dressed the hole in his arm.

Oakwood's finest were milling about, drinking coffee and sharing hushed versions of what had happened. Supporting the woman in their ranks one and all, Martin Rhodes included. Angie had put her life on the line today, not once, but twice, to save a fellow officer. After the day's events, nothing could stop her now from being their next sheriff.

The truth was, he couldn't wait with the guys. He couldn't be the smart-ass everyone would need him to be, so they could relax while they waited for word from the surgeon. He couldn't be anything but terrified.

"You told me it was okay to be scared." Maggie squeezed his hand until he looked at her. "As long as I didn't let being afraid keep me from making the decisions I had to make."

"What?"

"You said I could still be strong for Claire and Max, even if I was scared," said the girl who'd been a trouper over the last twenty-four hours. "Even if I'd messed up already. There's always a chance to make things right. You said that, remember? You and Angie will get your second chance. You have to."

"Maggie, I…" She couldn't know what she was saying. He pulled his hand free and stood. "I need some air."

Angie was in an operating room fighting for her life. Case in point why loving something only ended in pain. But somehow, because of all she'd become to him, and all she'd overcome, he couldn't stop craving what they might have together. If she'd only be okay. If she'd only pull through and give him one more chance to make things right…

Maggie grabbed his hand again. Pulling loose would have caused a scene.

"I saw how upset you were when Angie left last night," she insisted. "I know you're scared she won't make it, like—like your dad. But you don't have to wait here alone, Tony. You don't have to do everything by yourself—"

"I need some air." Away from his niece and her too-wise-for-her-years understanding. Not to mention the insanity of needing Angie to be okay, just for him.

He headed out of the waiting room, dodging bodies and questions as he turned toward the elevator.

This wasn't about him. It couldn't be about him.

He had no business hanging around like some important part of Angie's world, when he'd never seen a relationship through in his life. He had to forget those whispered words. He was Angie's friend, that's all. A good friend. The best. The guy she could depend on to make her laugh. The guy…

The guy she'd finally talked with about her ex and disastrous engagement. And made love to for the first time since she'd let the asshole convince her she wasn't gorgeous and sexy and every man's dream just the way she was, imperfections and all.

And then she'd gone and said she loved—

"Tony, hold up." A familiar grip from behind pulled him around.

Tony rounded on his brother.

Eric looked him over with a trained eye. "It's good to see you in one piece. I got over here as quick as I could. We had to secure the scene, and the mayor was beside himself about Garret. It— Damn, Tony. You—"

The vise of a bear hug that followed had Tony hugging back even harder.

"You okay?" Eric shoved him back, turning Tony slightly so he could check out the bandage on his upper arm. "How's your shoulder."

"It's nothing, man."

"It's not nothing, Tony." The grimness in Eric's

voice matched his eyes. "You saved my daughter and my wife, and even Carrinne's grumpy old grandfather. You saved my family. When I think of what could have happened—"

"Maggie's in the waiting room with the baby," Tony interrupted, the thought of his safe and healthy family wreaking havoc on his faltering control, as was the reminder that they'd be gone from his life in a matter of months. "She looks okay. She's a tough kid."

"She's amazing. Her mother, too. When the shooting started, I thought I'd lost all of you." His brother's expression shifted from relief to concern. "How's Angie? They couldn't tell me much when I called in on the way over."

"She's in surgery. They said she should be fine, but—" Tony couldn't force out the rest, so he gave looking straight through his brother his best shot.

The doctor had said the same terrifying word—*but*. They couldn't guarantee anything. They'd have to wait until they opened Angie up. All surgery comes with risks they sometimes couldn't contain.

Which meant Angie could still die.

God, please don't let her die.

The brown eyes looking deeply into his filled with shared memories. They weren't more than twenty feet away from the same E.R. their dad had been brought into after being shot in the line of duty. Only

Tony hadn't been there then. He'd been home with a neighbor, waiting for the bad news to come.

God, please don't let Daddy die.

"Angie's going to be okay," Eric assured him.

Tony could only nod. He lifted his gaze to the ceiling to ward off the tears that kept filling them. He fought off the memory of losing everything that had meant security and safety in his young life. And damn it to hell, if it didn't feel like it was happening again.

"The bullet got her liver and her spleen," he said. "Her blood pressure bottomed out on the ride over, but some kind of IV thing took care of it. They controlled the bleeding at the scene. So she should be okay, right?"

He swallowed the vile taste of not believing a word he was saying.

She had to be okay.

"Angie's not going anywhere, Tony." Eric's fatherly expression held a world of understanding. "You're going to get your chance to work things out with her. You'll see. Have a little faith."

Tony jerked away. His brother's assurances that things would magically work themselves out felt like a betrayal. Bullshit. Life didn't turn out that way, not Tony's life. And Eric used to understand that. Second chances were for other people. Making sure he had a good time and didn't care about the rest was what Tony's world had been about since he was a kid.

He had to get out of there.

He looked toward the waiting room. "Angie's family's freaked out of their minds. You should probably go sit with them until they hear something from the doc—"

"Do they know you love her?"

Tony's head snapped back. "Shut up, Eric. You don't know what you're talking about."

"Really? The two of you have been inseparable for months, and then some. You could lose your jobs, carrying on the way you have this week." He folded his arms, daring Tony to argue the point. "You've had each other's backs the last few days, and now you look like you're dying inside waiting to hear—"

"She took a bullet for me! What do you expect?"

"That's not all this is about, and you know it. The woman's gotten under your skin, and I'm inclined to be grateful. If she's gotten through that thick hide of yours this much—"

"So I feel like something's eating me from the inside out, is that what you want to hear?"

"At least you're feeling something."

L-love you.

"I can't be here anymore." Tony struck a path for the elevator that would race him to the ground-floor exit.

It was too much. Having her, losing her. Saving

his family, losing them, too. Being alone, and hating every damn second of it.

All of it was too much.

He should stay. He owed it to Angie. He should try and make the waiting easier for her family. He'd been where they were now, afraid but still hoping. Where he'd sworn he'd never be again. Then Angie had come along, understanding him, and fighting for him, then letting him go without any strings the way she'd promised she would. Right up until she'd said what he'd never let another woman say to him….

L-love you.

She'd been slipping further into unconsciousness with each word. She hadn't known what she was saying. And even if she had, he didn't deserve that kind of trust. He'd been scared too long. Running too long. All he had to offer was an empty shell of a man who'd forgotten how to feel anything real.

So the only decent thing he could do was get out of her way.

Please let her be okay, he prayed one last time as the elevator doors rolled open. He stumbled inside the empty car and stared at the floor.

"Running won't help, little brother," Eric said as the doors began to close. "What you need is down in that operating room. Walk away this time, and you'll regret it for the rest of your life."

CHAPTER EIGHTEEN

"T-TONY?" THE NAME ECHOED over and over in the cocoon insulating Angie's brain.

Oddly, she knew she was hurt, though she couldn't feel anything. And she was alone, but that wasn't right either. He'd been there before…but before what?

Didn't matter. He'd been there. But he wasn't now. Somehow she could tell, even though she couldn't open her eyes. There was light, but there wasn't really. Light on the other side of her eyelids that was muted. Shadowy. Like a memory of something she knew she should be remembering better.

Tony should be beside her, holding her. But hadn't she walked away, telling him it was okay? Hadn't she said she could handle whatever he had to give, and she wouldn't need more?

Then she'd said the unforgivable….

And now he was gone for good.

"Angie?" Lissa said from somewhere close by. "Angie wake up for me. We're all here, and you're going to be okay. The doctors stitched you up good as new, and everything's fine. You're a hero, sweetie. Wake up and talk to your fans."

A hero? Angie wanted to smile at her sister's words, but she couldn't. If Tony were there, she'd wake up. But he wasn't.

"Tony?" she asked one last time before letting herself slide back into the shadows.

He was gone, and he'd taken the light with him. Light she'd never realized she needed, until he'd shown her how to want it.

"YOU'RE A REAL PIECE OF WORK, you know that?" a brittle voice said from the door of Wilmington's totally trashed overseer's house.

Tony looked up from the couch and flinched at the anger hardening Melissa Warren's face. Without a word, he went back to what he was doing. The on-site team had finished their work hours ago and had sealed the scene. He'd been allowed in only to collect personal items. He'd packed the baby's few things already and was now gathering his and Maggie's extra clothes, stuffing them back into the duffel he'd brought them in. He was more than ready to leave the house and the events of the day behind.

He should be feeling better, now that he was away

from the hospital, and the emotions and memories that had overwhelmed him there. *Back to normal* was within his grasp.

Except, as Eric predicted, walking away hadn't blocked out what Tony knew he needed, or the memory of the woman he'd only hurt if he tried to keep her.

So much for a clean break.

"Your brother said you might be here." Melissa's eyes widened at the blood stains on the ancient rug beneath her feet.

"Look—" He reached for something polite to say as he zipped the duffel. "I don't know what you're doing here, but—"

"Your brother's been trying to reach you on your cell. Carrinne and your niece are on their way home now that Oliver's resting comfortably."

"Thanks for the update." He added enough bite to the words to move her out of his way as he brushed past. "It's nice of you to deliver the message."

"Angie's out of surgery, too. And she's asking for you." The toe of Lissa's sandal tapped the floor as he stumbled to a halt a few steps beyond her. "When I found out about you guys, I told her you'd ditch her, like you have every other woman in town. I just didn't figure you'd do it while she was fighting for her life—from injuries she got protecting your sorry hide."

"Is she all right?" he asked, absorbing Lissa's disdain without comment. He deserved it.

The woman shook her head in silence.

"Lissa, tell me Angie's okay, and I'll be out of her life for good. That's why you're here, right? To warn me off. So tell me she's going to be okay, and I'm gone."

Lissa's head kept shaking.

"She is okay, isn't she?" He tossed his bag aside and grasped Lissa's shoulders. The surgeon had been all optimism and promises when he'd spoken with the Carter family. But— "What's happened? What's wrong? She should be in recovery by now."

"Oh, the surgery's over." Lissa yanked free. "And she's doing fine in recovery. Unless you count the way she's crying in her sleep, calling for the person she's risked her career and her life for. Only he's too much of a bastard to stick around and finish what he started!"

Her words slapped Tony a hundred times harder than if she'd used her fist.

"She's better off without me there," he said, swamped by thoughts of a woman who'd seen through his laughter and his smiles to the crap beneath, then she'd promised to have his back, no matter what. "I'm no good for her, Lissa, and you know it. She has you and the rest of your family."

"She's suffering, you jerk. She wakes up more agitated each time. My family's not what she needs, and we haven't been for years. We've tried. For some reason I'm sure I don't understand, she needs you. No matter what I think about you, my sister's in love with you. She's begging for you." Lissa's tears fell as her voice rose. Her forefinger poked a steady beat into his breastbone. "So I don't care if you are a bastard, or if you've already decided to move on. You're going to march your butt right back to that hospital and hold Angie's hand until she's awake enough to come to her senses and throw you out of her life herself!"

Tony let Lissa's tantrum wash over him. Let her dig holes in his chest with her manicured fingernail. Let in the worst image he could pull from his nightmares. Angie, suffering and alone, needing him, and he wasn't there. The woman who'd invaded every part of his life, even his heart.

One last scathing stare from Lissa, and he headed for his truck.

Seeing Angie again was going to hurt like hell. Leaving again, when she came to her senses and realized she couldn't possibly love someone as messed up as he was, might just kill him. But he was going back for as long as Angie needed him.

...my sister's in love with you.

She's begging for you.

Cursing himself for a fool, he kicked into a sprint.

SOFT BUZZING SOUNDS floated through the air. Chirping and whirring. Familiar sounds, but not so familiar Angie could picture their source.

"Tony?" She struggled through layers of grogginess, trying to lift her eyelids. To make sense of the sluggish thoughts weighing them down.

Methodical, electronic noise answered back. She'd heard it all before, but where? Recognition flirted just beyond her reach. Clarity teased her, then escaped like a fuzzy sunbeam darting in and out of shadows. She sighed and stretched deeper into a soft blanket, until a distant pain—not as distant as before—shot up her left side.

"Lie still, darlin'," a warm voice said. An even warmer hand squeezed her fingers. "Do you want me to get your doctor?"

Hospital!

The pain and the sounds rushed together into a gaudy kaleidoscope of memories, shot through with the image of Sam Walker training a kill shot on—

"Tony!"

Walker had shot Tony. Now she'd never have the chance to say—

Love you.

Forcing her eyes open, she squinted into dim lighting. What time was it?

"It's close to seven," the voice beside her said.

Tony materialized out of her dreams and kissed the knuckles of the hand he was holding. Pressed it to that solid chest she loved to touch.

Her eyes filled. There was no stopping the tears.

He was okay. Everything was okay, only—

"It hurts...." The more awake she became, the more everything hurt.

What had happened? The last thing she remembered was firing on Walker, then lying in Tony's arms and saying—

"Oh, no." She winced.

She hadn't said it. Not the very last words she knew he wanted to hear.

She struggled to pull away. Pain ripped through her, setting her side on fire.

"Ah—" she gasped.

"Damn it!" Tony let her hand go and pressed something on the wall over her head. "The doctor will be here in a minute."

"No." She reached to stop him, but he'd moved too far away. "I'm fine."

"You're lucky to be alive. That bullet you took tore a hole through a lot of stuff." As she gazed into his haunted eyes, his hand reappeared to stroke her hair.

"You were in surgery for six hours while they stitched up God knows what. You…you could have—"

He broke eye contact to stare at the blanket tucked around her. Her hand hovered near his head, but she was afraid to touch him. Afraid he'd move away again if she tried.

"What have we here?" a doctor said as he and a nurse breezed into the room. "Look who's decided to wake up and tell me what a wonderful job I did knitting all her various parts back together. I'm Dr. Griffin, Ms. Carter. How are you feeling?"

"I'm…fine." Why was it so hard to think? To speak?

"She was in a lot of pain," Tony insisted as he backed away.

Angie fought not to grab for him. He was free to go. No strings. She'd insisted on it.

"Pain is entirely normal after abdominal surgery." Dr. Griffin read the gauges and monitors around her. "Everything's looking good."

Except she couldn't see Tony anymore. The nurse had stepped in between them to fiddle with the IV bag. The machine tracking Angie's heart rate blipped faster.

The doctor pulled a device from the blankets beside her head. "Press this button if the discomfort gets too bad. It's a self-administered morphine pump.

There's a cutoff. You can't give yourself too much, so enough being a hero for one day, okay? If you need it, take it. The nurse will check on you again in a bit."

Angie nodded as he handed her the gadget, and he and the nurse left. Her eyes trailed back to Tony. He'd backed himself into the corner, a scowl darkening his expression.

Wonderful. The sight of the man in scuffed boots, ratty jeans and a wrinkled T-shirt filled the entire room with wonderful.

Her chest squeezed against the pleasure-pain of having him there. The burning ache in her side scaled new heights. She started to press the button on the pump, then set it aside. She was confused enough without the fuzziness of pain meds.

"Don't be an idiot." Two strides of those long legs, and he was beside the bed. He thrust the device into her hand. "You heard the doctor. Use the medication if you need it. Stop trying to be a hero!"

She gaped at him. It was actually possible her jaw hit her chest.

"You're mad at me?"

"For putting yourself between me and a bullet, you're damn straight I'm mad at you!" The hands he'd squeezed into fists were visibly shaking.

"What are you doing here, if you're so pissed? Where's my family?"

"Down the hall. They'd be in here now, except there's a problem. Only one visitor is allowed in ICU at a time, and your sister was under the impression that you've been calling for me, and you wouldn't settle down until I came."

And here he was.

I'll get him, someone had said. *Don't worry, Angie. I'll get him.*

Lissa.

"I'm going to kill her." Angie stared at the man who was trapped exactly where she needed him. Exactly where she'd promised herself she wouldn't beg him to be. "I'm sorry, I—"

"Why did you do it?" One hand uncurled to take hold of hers, the gesture so gentle she gasped. "Why did you put yourself between Walker and me?"

The shadows in his eyes screamed he didn't really want to know.

"Everyone else—" She cleared her throat. He refused to let her hand slip away, so she stopped trying. "Are they okay?"

"Everyone's fine." He sat on the edge of the bed, the hostility fading from his voice. "Wilmington's a little banged up, and Maggie's still got a lot to deal with. But everyone's alive, thanks to you. Walker's gone." Satisfaction caressed his words. "And we've brought most of his family in for questioning. The

Mortons are flying in, so Max will be with them by the morning. You did a great job. The whole town's buzzing. You're a shoo-in for sheriff."

Job well done. Neat and tidy, exactly the way she liked it. She should be ecstatic. The future she'd wanted so badly was finally hers.

So why couldn't she shake the memory of how close she'd come to watching Tony die? And the realization that she'd give anything, even her own life, to prevent it. The peaceful new start she'd worked so hard for was impossible now. No matter how hard she denied it, her life didn't work, and it never would, unless Tony was there to share it with her.

She realized she was clinging to his hand. He wiped at the moisture seeping from the corners of her eyes.

"Why did you do it, Ange?" he whispered this time. "Why go and get yourself hurt like this...for me?"

"You know why. I...I'm sorry. I tried. I promised to walk away. To keep things light, but—"

"Screw keeping things light!" His kiss stole her next words. The moisture in his own eyes sent the blip monitoring her heartbeat into a minitantrum. "What you said, when I was holding you. That you— You didn't mean it, right? You couldn't mean it."

If he didn't believe her, he was safe, she realized. Maybe they both were.

But she didn't know what safe meant anymore.

"W-what if I did mean it?" she whispered, begging him with her eyes not to break her heart all over again.

"That's the shooting talking." He shook his head. "The surgery and the morphine."

"No, that's my heart, Tony." Even her sigh hurt. "The one that loves you no matter how much you don't want it to. Careless enough for you?"

"What about everything you've worked so hard for? You heard the doctor. You're a hero. The sheriff's office is yours. I'm a no-good playboy on suspension. The last person you need dragging you down—"

"You don't drag me down." She flashed back to their first kiss. To the impossible, out-of-control things he'd made her want and feel. "You've lifted me up, Tony Rivers. Shown me what I really need… I'm finally free, thanks to you."

"Free of that bastard, Peters?" He gave her a satisfied nod. "Good. If you're ready to move on and find someone who can make you happy, I'm glad."

"No, free of me. Free of protecting myself all the time. Free to need you for the rest of my life, and actually be happy about it, no matter what happens."

"You don't mean that." His anger was back, mixed with the fear that drove him to push everyone away. "You can't—"

"Why not?" She swallowed against the ringing in

her ears. "Because you might have to feel something, too?"

"You've got the wrong guy, darlin'. Haven't you figured that out?" He managed a chuckle. His fingers began to slide away. "I forgot how to feel things like love a lifetime ago."

"Bull." She held onto his hand with every speck of strength she had left. "You've got the biggest heart in the county, no matter how hard you fight to hide it."

"Don't you think I want to love you back! It's killing me, knowing I can't give you what you need. I'd only hurt you if I tried, Angie. Worse than Freddie did."

"No, you won't." She smiled through her tears, his angry admission sweeter than a thousand kisses. "You'll love me for the rest of your life, just like you love your brother and his family. Face it. You can't help it. The only way you can hurt me is by refusing to accept what I see in you every time we're together."

The room grew silent. She could feel his longing to believe her. To finally believe in himself.

Come on, Tony. Be careless just one more time.

"What—" He leaned closer. His lips caressed hers again. "What do you see, Angie?"

"A man who's strong enough to follow his heart when it counts, screw the risks. A man who's good for me. Who's everything I'll ever need."

He framed her face with his hands and gazed deep

into her eyes, his soul open and there for her to read. Only for her. "Nothing on this earth is good enough for you, darlin'."

"Except you."

"You really believe that?"

"You bet your sweet ass I do," she said, relishing the beauty of his favorite comeback. Praying the glimmer of trust in his eyes would catch hold and thrive. "I'm done hiding from what I want, Tony. No more playing it safe. Me and you together. It's worth fighting for, don't you think?"

"Because... Because you love me?" The tentative hope in his words broke her heart all over again. Only this time, love spilled through the cracks, not tears.

"Yes, I love you."

"You nearly got yourself killed for me." He kissed her again, his lips lingering this time.

"But I'm still here. Still loving you. And I'm not going anywhere."

Amazing how it was easier to say each and every time.

Tony buried his face in her hair, her dream come true holding her close as if he meant to stay. And when he pulled back, his sexy lips curled into the smile she'd bet her future on.

"You really are crazy," he said. "Only a crazy

woman would throw in with a misfit like me. But God help me, Angie Carter, no matter how hard I try not to, I love you, too."

EPILOGUE

"DO YOU, ANTHONY GERALD RIVERS, take this woman, Angela Grace Carter, to be your loving wife, to…"

The words washed over Angie in a wave of dreamlike perfection. Impossible perfection for a woman who'd sworn her life was going to be so very different than where she'd ended up—dressed in the ultrafeminine gown her mother had insisted on, holding hands with the love of her life, standing before a judge who was uniting their souls forever, their families and the rest of Oakwood looking on.

"I do," Tony said. He squeezed her fingers, then let go to wipe happy tears from the corner of her eye.

"And do you, Angela Grace Carter, take this man, Anthony Gerald Rivers, to be your loving husband, to…"

It was her turn to dab at Tony's eyes. She covered the motion by brushing back his almost-too-long hair.

They'd agreed on a hastily planned wedding, before Eric and his family's move next week. The ceremony was nothing more than a formality for them. Their secondhand hearts had become one that afternoon two months ago in her hospital room.

"…till death do you part?" the minister finished.

"I do," she said through a smile Tony mirrored back.

"Then by the power vested in me by this fair city, I pronounce you husband and wife."

The room erupted in applause, drowning out the minister saying, "You may now kiss the bride."

Not that Tony needed any prompting.

He drew her hand to his heart, a tribute to all they'd overcome for this miracle to unfold. He tenderly kissed her fingertips. Then not nearly as gently, he hauled her into his arms for the consuming kiss of a man who'd slept alone in his bachelor bed last night.

Spectators hooted and hollered, drowning out Tony's groan. Overflowing with the promise of the day, the future happiness it didn't hurt to believe in anymore, Angie began to laugh. A perfect kind of laugh, because Tony was chuckling right along with her.

"Happy?" He glanced over her shoulder at the two rows of deputies in attendance, from Pineview as well as Oakwood.

He'd interviewed at the adjoining county's sheriff's department the same day his suspension had cleared in Oakwood. He'd become part of the

Pineview staff a full day before the final vote had been tallied, and Angie had officially won Oakwood's sheriff's position.

"I never thought I could be this happy." She pulled his head back down so she could reach his lips again.

"Get a room," came a rumbling jibe from the crowd wearing their dress uniforms and Sunday best.

"Good idea." Tony grabbed her hand, poised to make good on his threat to escape early for their honeymoon through the choir-loft door.

"I don't think so, Mr. Rivers." Angie dug in, prepared to wrestle him to the ground, wedding dress and all.

"I did the tux," he growled. "And I kept my hands off you last night. Now let's get out of here."

"No. We're finishing this. No more running." She turned, dragging him around with her. Linking her arm with his, she smiled at the crowd. Took her bouquet from Lissa, her maid of honor, as expected.

"Ladies and gentlemen, I present to you Tony and Angie Carter Rivers," the minister announced on cue.

More applause sounded as Tony obligingly escorted her down the aisle, shaking his best man's hand as they went—Eric was beaming right along with his wife. Too many pats on the back, hugs and kisses to count, and they'd reached the front of the church and their waiting limo—rented all the way from an Atlanta dealer, courtesy of none other than Oliver Wilmington himself.

"Finally, a fast getaway." Tony swept her into his arms and charged for the car, outrunning the cheering crowd at their heels.

Angie giggled at his playfulness, certain he was the sexiest man on the face of the earth as he slowed their escape long enough to gently tuck her flowing veil and train around her. Once he'd jogged to his side of the car, tossed off his tuxedo jacket, settled beside her and shouted, "Go!" to the driver, she pounced, throwing her arms around her husband's broad shoulders.

"Gotcha," she said, clinging to the overwhelming rightness of thinking of this man as her husband, of herself as married.

Tony filled his hands with as much of the dress and her as he could hold. "Who's got who, Madam Sheriff?"

And then they were kissing, forgetting the crowd they were leaving behind and the driver whisking them toward the Rivers home for the reception Carrinne and Maggie had insisted on orchestrating.

Forget about hiding from the past. Forget about the nightmares and worries they might never completely banish. Forget about everything but now. That's what they'd promised each other her first night home from the hospital, when he'd gotten down on his knee in her perfect-for-one apartment and slipped a ring on her finger.

"I love you with all my heart, Angie Carter," Tony whispered in her ear. "How did that happen? What on earth are you doing married to a no-good bum like me? Didn't your mama teach you better?"

She sighed, resting her head on his shoulder, rubbing a finger across the ring of gold she'd slid on his finger. "You're just too persistent. You wore me down."

His chuckle filled her with the light that had captured her heart long before she was brave enough to call the feeling anything but friendship.

"That'll be my story when anyone asks. I'm all about sweet-talking reluctant women and getting them to commit." He tipped her chin up for a soft kiss that belied his bad-boy words. His brown eyes adored her. "Of course, we'll always know who had the guts to dream all this up."

Proud of them both for grabbing hold of tomorrow and refusing to let go, Angie ran a shaking hand through her husband's soft hair.

Her husband.

"As if I could do anything else, once you turned that devilish smile on me," she said. "You're exactly where I should be, every second of every day. You made giving you up impossible, every time you made me laugh. You made me want more, and more, until all I wanted was you."

"Damn straight," he said, catching her close.

"'Cause I'm all you're going to get from now on. Now let's go drink some champagne, eat some cake, kiss a few cheeks and get the hell out of town so we can move on to the good stuff!"

OPEN SECRET

by Janice Kay Johnson

HSR #1332

Three siblings, separated after their parents'
death, grow up in very different homes,
lacking the sense of belonging that family
brings. The oldest, Suzanne, makes up her
mind to search for her brother and sister,
never guessing how dramatically her
decision will change their lives.

Also available:
LOST CAUSE (June 2006)

On sale March 2006

Available wherever Harlequin books are sold!

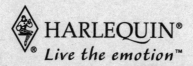

Live the emotion™

Detective Maggie Skerritt is on the case again!

Maggie Skerritt is investigating a string
of murders while trying to establish her
new business with fiancé Bill Malcolm.
Can she manage to solve the case
while moving on with her life?

Spring*Break*

by *USA TODAY* bestselling author

CHARLOTTE DOUGLAS

HARLEQUIN®

N^ext™

Available March 2006
TheNextNovel.com

HN33

You always want
what you don't have

Dinah and Dottie are two sisters who grew up
in an imperfect world. Once old enough to make
decisions for themselves, they went their separate
ways—permanently. Until now. Will their reunion
seventeen years later during a series of crises
finally help them create a perfect life?

My Perfectly
Imperfect Life

Jennifer Archer

HARLEQUIN®

Ne_xt™

Available March 2006
TheNextNovel.com

HARLEQUIN®
Super Romance®

*A compelling and emotional story
from a critically acclaimed writer.*

How To
Get Married

by Margot Early

SR #1333

When Sophie Creed comes home to
Colorado, one person she doesn't want to
see is William Ludlow, her almost-husband
of fifteen years ago—or his daughter, Amy.
Especially since Sophie's got a secret that
could change Amy's life.

On sale March 2006
Available wherever Harlequin books are sold!

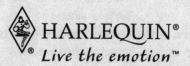

HARLEQUIN®
Live the emotion™